A TIME TO BE BORN
AND A TIME TO DIE

A Time to be Born
and
a Time to Die

STEPHANIE
PLOWMAN

THE BODLEY HEAD
LONDON SYDNEY
TORONTO

For the girls I taught
who were sorry to see me go

© Stephanie Plowman 1975
ISBN 0 370 10952 X
Printed in Great Britain for
The Bodley Head Ltd
9 Bow Street, London WC2E 7AL
by Unwin Brothers Ltd, Woking
Set in Monotype Imprint
by Gloucester Typesetting Co., Ltd
First published 1975.

Contents

Author's Note

I shot an arrow — is based on the examination of the death of William II by the late Duncan Grinnell-Milne in *The Killing of William Rufus* (David & Charles). I am very glad to acknowledge my debt to Mr Grinnell-Milne, and am grateful to his son for his permission to set down his father's theories in a short story.

The Guillotine and its Servants by G. Lenôme, alluded to in *The High Cost of Dying*, was published in England by Messrs Hutchinson.

General Dobrorolsky's pamphlet, *Die Mobilmachung der Russischen Armee 1914*, was published in Berlin in 1921.

Three cadets went out to Tsarskoe Selo on the eve of the Revolution, as narrated in *Incubation*, and with the results described. No further details about them are known, however.

Finally, had it not been for *Hindenburg, the Wooden Titan* by Sir John Wheeler-Bennett (Macmillan Ltd.), the last story would never have been written.

I

'I Shot an arrow-'

(Ponthieu and England, 1100 AD)

The night before the hunt the Lord of Poix dreamed, curiously, of cats. It may have been that the patter of the rain that was falling as he drowsed into sleep caused him to hear in his dreams the quick light pad of cats' paws, but dream of cats he did, and even when he awoke, it being still dark, he seemed to hear them scampering and scuffling.

There had been four cats in the dream. Two sat one on each side of him, one had come rubbing against him, much to the discomfort of the Lord of Poix, who had never liked these beasts; the fourth sat aloof, staring at him as if it were assessing him for some purpose, but then quite suddenly it had padded off, and its three fellows, as if they had received a signal, followed it. But before they parted from the Lord of Poix, the caresses of the beast that had fawned on him became a brief, savage clawing, so that the Lord of Poix, awaking, and still seeming to hear the furtive noise of their retreat, clapped his hand to his ankle, and was surprised to find no blood there.

He was also ashamed to find that his heart was beating very quickly indeed—because of a quartet of the creatures he had hitherto viewed with genial contempt. His wife Alice had a white cat, but the animal was wise enough to realise the distaste the Lord of Poix felt for it, and usually kept out of his way.

'Really,' thought the Lord of Poix, sitting up and yawning, 'I can't recall as much about the beast as I can of the picture in the book Brother Martin used to show me.'

He remembered that page in the bestiary very well—could,

indeed, remember the very writing of it. The limner had already done his work; there sat the cat, with its supercilious stare, and beneath it Brother Martin, seated at his high desk with its quill pens and trimming knife, and a good supply of iron-gall ink, wrote with steady strokes, and then read what he had written to the small boy standing respectfully beside him. 'It has earned the name of CAT because it catches and entraps unwary things —that is *a captura*. But it may also well be that this name has been given it because it watches, and lies in wait for its prey (*captat*).'

Suddenly the Lord of Poix became aware that he had not, after all, imagined hearing rustlings and movement outside the door. But it was human movement. He leapt up, dragged his cloak about him, ran to the door of his cubicle. He had never felt really at ease in this, his first visit to a country occupied by his hosts for less than his own lifetime.

He flung open the door and came face to face with his brother-in-law, Eudo, husband of his wife's elder sister, Rohese. Eudo looked wild-eyed enough, but the reason was a purely personal one, he being *dapifer*, or cup-bearer to the King, and the commotion, it appeared, having been caused by the King's sudden indisposition. 'He must have caught a chill—or it was too much venison last night.'

'Yes,' agreed the Lord of Poix, 'it couldn't have been too much wine—he's an abstemious man.'

Eudo looked startled. 'For God's sake, don't say anything about the wine!' he whispered.

The Lord of Poix apologised awkwardly. 'You all know how Alice always laughs and says I'm slow-witted,' he concluded. (Tactless indeed to talk about over-indulgence in wine to the King's cup-bearer, even though privately he felt Eudo's reaction was exaggerated. The cup-bearer was hardly to blame for the quantity his master drank.)

Eudo grinned momentarily. 'Yes—' he began, but then changed his tone. 'I must go to him,' he said. 'You can go back to bed—lucky devil.'

His brother-in-law did, but was scarcely convinced of his good fortune. More than ever he wished he had not crossed the Channel. If the King were ill, the hunt next day would be called off; that would give him the chance to make his excuses and go home—perhaps after paying a brief visit to the manor of Langham in Essex with which he had been enfeoffed on marriage by his father-in-law. But then he decided he would not visit Langham. He had held it so long without ever setting eyes on it, there was no hurry now—indeed, all the hurry came from this obscure but infinitely troubling feeling that he should go home at once, back to his young son Hugh, and his wife Alice. Dear Alice, so simple and direct in thought and manner, and so unlike her brothers, clever men, always in the past condescending to Alice's husband, and therefore privately surprising him that one of them (not Gilbert, the Earl, it was true, but Roger, who was almost equally formidable) should have ridden from his home at Brionne to convey the invitation, had borne down the Lord of Poix's protests that he did not want to go, and finally had accompanied him over to England.

The royal hunting party, as the King had remarked the night before, was more like a de Clare family party—Earl Gilbert, his brother Roger, his brother-in-law Eudo, and his other brother-in-law, Walter Tirel, Lord of Poix, a quiet, kindly man, earnest benefactor of Holy Church, with no wish to make a great name for himself—or, indeed, as he himself would have been the first to admit, the ability to achieve renown. Like his wife Alice, he was something of a laughing-stock to the rest of her family of strenuous, ambitious brothers and sisters. The only talent possessed by the gentle numbskull from Poix was his gift for fine shooting with the long bow.

Even the King of England had heard of Walter Tirel's skill with the bow, said Roger as they had sat sipping spiced wine after dinner. 'Ah, brother,' Alice had replied, 'but that must be because you or Gilbert have told him so.' She had looked gratefully at her brother, then affectionately towards her husband.

9

Roger replied irritatedly that it might well be so. He often sounded irritable when he talked to his sister, but on this occasion the edge to his voice was even more pronounced.

It rained during the crossing of the Channel, but then it had rained all that summer. Roger became his usual taciturn self, the affability he had recently shown his brother-in-law having been completely uncharacteristic. Walter Tirel, that kindly man, fell into conversation with another passenger, a merchant. The merchant was gloomy. All the crops in England were ruined by the rain. But, then, everyone had known that 1100 would be a bad year for England. There had been warning enough in the previous November—had his lordship not heard of the great tide which, on the day of the new moon, had swept up the Thames, destroying houses, whole villages even, and carrying away to destruction men, sheep, oxen?

'Why did you talk to that vulgar fool?' demanded Roger, a short time later.

'He was interesting,' said Walter Tirel, and then, since Roger's sudden appearance at his side and stammered question were reminiscent of the awkward way in which he himself, having been at fault, would blurt out anything in an attempt to restore things to a friendly footing again, he tried to meet his brother-in-law halfway. Smilingly he said, 'You're taking me to a dangerous place, brother. I've half a mind to find another ship the moment we land, and go home again.'

Roger gaped at him, his face suddenly ashen. 'I believe the poor devil's seasick,' thought Tirel, trying not to be pleased because he, who had never crossed the Channel, felt no malaise whatsoever, whereas that experienced traveller, his brother-in-law, looked decidedly unhealthy at the present moment. 'I was not serious!' he said contritely. 'I told him that I should not have to worry about tides and such things, being safe enough in this New Forest made by your King's father.'

After this he told Roger what the merchant had said to him about the Great Tide. Roger listened with flattering interest, and at the end smiled and actually clapped his brother-in-law on the shoulder. 'That was all?' he demanded.

'All,' replied the honest Tirel, 'except that he took me up when I spoke about being safe in the New Forest. That isn't so safe a place, he said—after all the King's young nephew Richard was accidentally shot there in May of this year. I hadn't known about it, so he told me. It does seem a shocking affair,' continued Tirel, his professional anger aroused. 'An attendant aiming at a stag, missing and hitting his master! I've never heard of such bungling. From what this good fellow was telling me, there was a regular outcry after it—'

Roger said, 'You will not mention that matter again!'

Meeting the glare in his eyes, Tirel could only nod dumbly. And he could only nod dumbly when Roger said, 'Give me your word you will not mention it again,' before going to stand not too far off at the ship's side, gazing in sullen menace at his brother-in-law.

Tirel himself felt somewhat sullen. Did Roger think him a fool? But, ready as ever to find extenuation for others, he reminded himself that Roger, like Gilbert, would be on tenterhooks lest any connection of theirs said or did anything to antagonise the King—they themselves could not be wholly at ease (at least he himself would not be!) in the King of England's company, having been twice in rebellion against him since his accession thirteen years before—once the year after William became King, the second time only five years before. Twice they had been pardoned; the King would not condemn loyalty, even loyalty to his enemies, but—'Well, *I* should not feel at ease in such a situation,' thought Walter Tirel, 'and I must remember to do nothing to endanger them. No wonder Roger is ill-tempered.'

Strangely, perhaps, Tirel had no fear of meeting the King of England himself. Possibly the nickname had something to do with it. Tirel knew other men nicknamed '*le roux*', '*le rouquin*', and the nickname had always carried with it the smack of affection. The thick-set red-haired King did not terrify, even when he became excited and stammered so violently he was almost inarticulate. His grey eyes, flecked with brown spots, sometimes had a jeering expression, but to Tirel himself he showed greater friendliness than Tirel received from his own relatives by marriage; Tirel felt at home with him. He was reminded of a mastiff his father had once owned, reddish-haired, gruff-voiced, formidable.

He did not, however, feel at home with the King's younger brother. Where the elder was rough, the younger was sleek, smooth of face and hair. His dark eyes sneered even if his small mouth smiled, showing very white teeth. He said little; he had a gift for keeping in the background. Even his movements seemed silent to the point of stealthiness.

If Henry chose to remain in the background, another brother was very much in the foreground of people's minds even if he were many miles away. Gilbert de Clare had taken it upon himself the evening after Tirel's arrival to carry on from where Roger had left off, and instruct his brother-in-law as to the matters not to be discussed before the King. To a dead nephew one added a living brother. Duke Robert of Normandy, the King of England's elder brother, was on his way home from the Crusades, having married in Italy. Tirel protested mildly that he knew as much. Gilbert rarely frowned, having a control of his facial muscles that his brother-in-law found far more intimidating than the stammering grimaces of the English King, but on this occasion his heavy brows contracted ominously. 'There may be trouble when the Duke returns to Normandy,' he remarked coldly.

'They say he is expected back in September,' said Tirel, 'or even sooner. But why should there be trouble? There was a treaty of friendship and inheritance signed by the brothers, was there not—King and Duke to be each other's heir should either die childless? And that was reaffirmed when the Duke pawned Normandy to the King to raise the money to go on crusade.'

Gilbert replied that Duke Robert was now married to a bride not only beautiful but bringing him a large dowry, more than enough to redeem Normandy. 'So one does not mention the Duke in the King's presence.'

But even Gilbert could be wrong, thought Tirel with some satisfaction later that evening. The King himself raised the matter at dinner. 'Robert the bridegroom,' he shouted cheerfully, 'Robert no doubt soon to be the father—father of an heir to *my* kingdom and *his* duchy. Well,' he guffawed, 'that's a game two can play—eh, Henry?' He winked at his brother, who looked down and made no reply. 'What's the matter?' demanded the King. 'Lost your tongue?'

'Lost my appetite, rather,' said his brother. 'I'm sick of venison, eager for the taste of mutton again.'

'Buck's in season from the end of June,' said the King. 'We eat venison. There's plenty of it, and in a couple of weeks' time I may be wanting the Saxons behind me as much as I wanted them at the beginning of my reign.' He turned to Tirel and explained. 'Saxons don't like killing their best calves and lambs for meat—they like to keep 'em for breeding. They kill off the old stock before the winter, but otherwise it's cheese for them through most of the year, and fowl and fish and suchlike. I'll tell you something, Tirel. A year after I became King I had to call out the Saxon *fyrd*—every man able to bear arms. Old Bishop Wulfstan of Worcester raised the Midlands for me while I concentrated on Kent. Afterwards I asked him what I could do for him. "Lord King," he said, "the people's wealth depends on their herds, and they want to keep the best stock for breeding. Then your cooks come around demanding those best beasts. That's what keeps hatred alive today—not the thought of the Englishmen your father slaughtered at Senlac and in the north, but the slaughter of the sheep to become what you Normans call *mutton*. If you want help from the English, leave them their flocks and herds." Which,' concluded the King, 'I haven't forgotten.'

Gilbert's face remained as impassive as ever, but Roger's was not so well schooled. Catching the flicker of expression on his brother-in-law's face, Tirel wondered how the King could not

also have remembered that in that rebellion the de Clares had
been against him.

Tirel and Roger de Clare had landed at Southampton on
July 27. From Southampton they rode to Winchester, where the
King was staying. The rain had stopped soon after their land-
ing; the King, greeting Tirel with boisterous good humour,
hailed him as the bringer of good weather and, no doubt, good
luck. 'The rain stopped two weeks ago for a day or two—I
cursed our bad luck, I can tell you, that it was still mid-July and
the Fence Month.* But now, if the weather stays good, we can
ride out on Monday.'

Not before, although Tirel had landed on a Friday. But the
29th was the feast of St Peter-ad-Vinculam, and it seemed that the
King, for all his jeers at the priesthood, went to Mass often
enough. Tirel was as inexpert at concealing his thoughts as his
brother-in-law was adept; Robert Fitzhamon, the King's oldest
and most loyal friend, eager, like any friend, to clear up any mis-
conceptions of a denigrating nature, explained quietly to the
newcomer that his master had some good friends among the
clergy—there was, for example, Abbot Serlo of Gloucester.
Conversation with Fitzhamon was soothing; one did not have
to be eternally on one's guard.

So, after the 29th, they had set out from Winchester, the
weather being favourable. It took some two and a half hours to
cover the twenty miles between Winchester and the royal hunting lodge; the road was atrocious, treachery itself in the best of
weathers, with deep ruts everywhere.

The sun, beginning to sink into the west, shone directly in
their eyes as they came to the hunting lodge, so that it was impossible for Tirel to see it clearly, or to distinguish the foresters
and servants who came running out as they rode through the
encircling palisade, to fall on their knees as the royal party
approached—a black bulk in the background, black kneeling

* When the does were calving, the close season for deer hunting. The
close season ended on July 20.

14

figures in the foreground to whom the King called out a bluff greeting.

'Ah, Walter,' said the King, turning in the saddle, 'here is a man who'll be a good friend to you, Ranulf des Aix. The Chief Hunter'll look after you very well.'

Tirel, dismounting stiffly, expressed due gratitude.

To his pleasure, and something to his surprise, next morning his brothers-in-law let him go off with the Chief Hunter into the Forest without either declaring that one of them would accompany him or, indeed, warning him against any foolish speech. They themselves were in attendance on the King, who had business to transact; news had come overnight that the King's brother was even nearer than had been thought.

'But affairs of State, thank God, do not concern you and me,' said Ranulf to Tirel. 'Who'd be a king?' And he burst out laughing. He had an infectious laugh, and Tirel joined in. From the start he had taken to the Chief Hunter, a man with a most frank, open face made remarkable by eyes of the darkest blue Tirel had ever seen. The visitor envied his new-found friend's steady gaze; he himself, he knew, blinked in woeful confusion when confronted with any unforeseen situation.

They rode through the Forest. Ranulf talked with a knowledge that impressed Tirel even if he could not be enthusiastic about what he saw. For he did not like the Forest. It was a furzy waste, a wilderness, open heath, bogs as well as dense woods of beech or oak where the sun never penetrated even at noon on a July day and where shadow stretched black as ink.

They met two keepers, Saxons, but with some knowledge of Norman French. Ranulf spoke to them sharply and contemptuously. 'Slow, superstitious fools,' he said to Tirel, not bothering to lower his voice. 'But they know their job,' Tirel protested mildly. Ranulf regained his good humour. 'Yes, they have their uses,' he said, laughing. 'Even the biggest of fools can have his uses.'

The King did not hunt that day or the next, being engrossed with business. On the third day they rode out, but within minutes the sky clouded; through the afternoon and evening the rain streamed ceaselessly from a grey sky. The delay, frustration, postponement of carefully worked-out arrangements, eroded even Ranulf's good humour, eroded it enough to produce a bellow of rage from the King. What was said by the Chief Hunter at noon on the third day, Tirel did not know, being at some distance from where the King sat, but he saw the sudden transformation of the jocular accessible host who had never stood upon his dignity into a master boiling with furious passion. In his rage he stammered incoherently; all that the embarrassed Tirel could distinguish was the last shout, accompanied by a fist crashing on the table: 'As I have told you before!'

Tirel, that kindly man, was glad that Ranulf's back was to him, sparing him the sight of his friend's face.

And so on to the morning of August 2.

The King, having been indisposed, had not fallen asleep until dawn, but had made good use of his wakefulness, sending for more lights, keeping his clerks as well as his Chamberlain with him, and dictating letter after letter, and in the morning, although he got up much later than usual, he applied himself to serious business. Tirel, stretching his legs in the courtyard, heard in snatches of conversation mention of a letter to the King of Scotland. But, in the late afternoon, the King decided he would, after all, ride out in the early evening. 'Time enough for you, Ranulf?' he asked with a grin.

'Time enough, my lord,' said Ranulf, smiling.

At the early dinner the King's mood seemed to be one of great satisfaction, Tirel remarked to Ranulf. 'Certainly he eats and drinks more than usual,' said Ranulf in a non-committal voice; his eyes moved from the King, belching, wiping his hand across his mouth, then lifting his cup again, to the King's brother, eating delicately, sipping fastidiously. 'He's like a cat,' thought Tirel, remembering how Henry had flown into a rage the night before when a spot of wine fell on to his tunic sleeve. Someone else had once said that Henry was like a cat—who was it? Why, his own wife, Alice, quoting what her father had heard Henry's own father say. 'Normandy to Robert, England to William—no land for Henry, but there's no need to shed tears for Henry—he's like a cat, throw him any way you like and he'll land on his feet.'

Ranulf excused himself before the ending of the meal, and went away to see that all was ready. He reappeared when the King was pulling on his boots: a smith craved audience, wishing to present the King with six new arrows, specially made. The King, in perfect good humour again, said he would see the man, accepted the arrows, and complimented the maker on his skill. The smith, so nervous he could scarcely speak, mumbled his thanks and withdrew.

They were, indeed, excellent arrows—'As good as anything your guest has seen in Ponthieu, my lord,' said Ranulf, in tearing high spirits with the prospect of action before him.

'What do you say, Walter?' asked the King.

Tirel fingered the arrows lovingly, and nodded.

'Here,' said the King, 'I keep four for myself and give two to you. The man who shoots to kill should have the best.'

'Ranulf, my lord,' began Tirel, 'is as good a shot as I, if not better, so the arrows should—'

But the King's attention was distracted. Robert Fitzhamon came in to say that a monk had come with an urgent message from Abbot Serlo of Gloucester. The King burst out laughing. 'Has his new Abbey, consecrated only a fortnight ago, fallen down then? But let him come in—if he keeps the message short.' At the same time Gilbert and Roger were at Tirel's elbow. 'Hold your tongue, you fool. He's been pleased to be generous; do you want him to fly into a rage by turning down his gift?'

'But Ranulf is as good a shot as I, and it was really on his prompting that the King thought of making me the gift—'

'Hold your fool of a tongue, for God's sake.'

17

The monk, Fitzhamon was saying, wished to see the King in private.

The King laughed. 'What—does he want me to confess my sins to him? Get rid of him, Robert.'

Fitzhamon bowed, went out. The King shouted for more wine, proclaiming he was thirsty. Fitzhamon came back as his master was draining the cup; the monk had dreamed that the Church had called to God for vengeance on the King. The King laughed again. 'Just like a monk!' he said. 'He's dreaming for money. Tell him to go away, Robert—and give him a hundred shillings.'

But when Fitzhamon got to the courtyard, the monk had already gone. Those who had talked to the man said he had seemed disturbed. First he had insisted on seeing the King alone; then, when Fitzhamon had gone to the King with this message, the monk had cried out, as if to himself, 'But I *must* see him, alone or not!' One of the men-at-arms had told him there was little chance of his seeing the King alone, he should be glad to have the chance of talking to him at all, as he was busy discussing hunting prospects with great lords like his brother and Earl Gilbert de Clare. At this the monk had abruptly gone away.

'I thought Serlo had more sense,' commented the King: 'I thought him a good old fellow, above sending me stories of the dreams of a snoring monk.'

Fitzhamon shrugged, dismissing the episode, then again tried to persuade his master both because of the lateness of the time and his recent sickness to give up the idea of hunting that day.

Ranulf, Eudo and the de Clares had all gone down to the courtyard, laughing, to see if they could find the monk. But when Tirel and the King's brother joined them, they reported he was not to be found. They stood impatiently in the courtyard, chafing, frustrated. 'For God's sake, what's the delay?' Gilbert de Clare asked his brother-in-law. Tirel replied that Fitzhamon was trying to persuade the King to give up all thought of hunting for the day. The King's brother gave a slight exclamation, and went back into the lodge. A few minutes later he was at the window with the King. Ranulf, hardily, began chaffing the King. So did Gilbert. They wanted to start; was the King afraid of the monk's dream? The King was undecided; Fitzhamon drew him back into the room. Ranulf boldly ordered that the horses should be brought round, and the tufter hounds.

The King looked out of his window again, and decided to hunt. It was nearly half past six.

The King came down in his russet tunic, grinning at the cheers and laughter with which his friends greeted him. 'Well, Ranulf,' he said amiably, 'you've caught me! What have you arranged?'

'We've only two hours of daylight left to us in which we can do anything useful, my lord. If we beat the woods towards Canterton Manor, they're less than a mile off. We could be in position within half an hour.'

'Right,' said the King. 'Take me to the place you've marked out for me, and then look after Walter.'

They left the palisade and rode along a short track between the trees down to an old road which they followed to the west. There were a dozen riders, and as many attendants and foresters, together with a small armed guard, to take charge of the horses when the riders had dismounted.

After they had gone some three hundred yards there was a halt while the first party—the de Clares and the King's brother —took a track leading to the right, towards Canterton. Two hundred yards further on there was another halt for Fitzhamon with William of Breteuil, Keeper of the Treasury, to take another path branching to the right. The King and Tirel went on with their attendants under Ranulf's guidance, continuing no great distance on horseback to a point where a bridlepath dipped down into a hollow.

'We dismount here,' said Ranulf, and explained in a low, rapid voice that with a light north-west wind blowing this was the best position obtainable—an open space and a glade to the west, woods on either side within a range of fifty yards. The deer were known to be lying in a thicket to the west; the beaters, working from up wind, would drive them into the open space.

They left their horses. The evening woods were now so still that the tramp of a horse, the jingle of harness was unthinkable. For a quarter of a mile, and with increasing caution, they made their way on foot to the positions chosen by Ranulf. The party now consisted of the King, Tirel and Ranulf, the King's personal attendant, Ranulf's, the attendant assigned to Tirel by his brother-in-law ('No need to bring your own man, very likely he'd be more of a hindrance than anything else') and a forest guide for each—Tirel's was hardly more than a boy, spoke little or no Norman-French, and looked terrified. But he knew the Forest and the ways of the deer, Ranulf had explained, and walked as warily as a fox.

They left the King standing beside a great oak; once Ranulf had set Tirel in his position, he would return to his master and give the signal (by hand so as not to break silence and alarm the deer) to the Chief Keeper to send the beaters closing in. The Chief Keeper himself was at the south-western corner of the northern wood, just out of sight of any deer driven into the glade but within twenty yards of the first man of the extended line of beaters.

'*I* can't see where he's positioned,' the King had muttered. 'How can he see you?'

'I shall have to leave you, my lord, and move—say about twenty yards to the west,' said Ranulf. 'There—towards the edge of the grove.'

To reach Tirel's position they moved at first through trees so dense that Tirel could not see more than a dozen yards in any direction. He was glad when they came to a veiled kind of brightness and then a thick growth of hazels, and, beyond it, the open clearing, grass, some bracken, with the luminous evening light pouring down.

'Here,' whispered Ranulf. 'Under this tree.'

Tirel, who had had it in mind since they left the hunting lodge, took the opportunity to offer his friend the two special arrows given him by the King. Ranulf replied no, quite violently. 'One, then,' whispered Tirel. Ranulf took the proffered arrows, and gave them to Tirel's attendant. 'See that your master uses them,' he said.

'Have I offended you?' stammered Tirel.

Ranulf turned to him, smiling. 'Do I seem offended?'

He did not. His blue eyes glowed with excitement—or was it nervousness? Stung by contrition Tirel said, 'I should not keep you—the King's waiting.'

'Yes,' said Ranulf, 'the King's waiting.' He gave a glittering smile and went off noiselessly. Tirel, left alone, became aware of minor discomforts; there was little birdsong now so late in the day, but there was a great buzzing of flies, a long-drawn-out whining sound, and there was an unpleasant smell, sickly-sweet, decaying, everywhere about him. He discovered the tree beneath which he stood was an elder. Because of the extraordinary weather that year it had been slow in flowering and the blossom was still brown and rotting on the boughs. Tirel disliked elder trees. He was a devout man and had heard that the Cross had been made of elder wood. And had not Brother Martin once told him that it had been on an elder tree that Judas, the arch-traitor, had hanged himself?

And then the hunt began.

There would be agonised attempts enough by Tirel in the future to recall precisely what happened then, but it was never possible. He only knew positively that two stags came crashing into the glade from two different paths some fifty yards apart, and made for the south. The first came from the more westerly path, sixty odd yards away. It was a difficult target, head-on. But the light was good, and as it advanced he waited, special arrow nocked on bowstring, hoping for a flank shot at closer range when the beast came into the centre of the glade.

Out of the corner of his eye he saw the other stag break

cover, closer to the King. 'He must wait—too difficult a shot,' Tirel thought automatically. 'Then, if he grazes it, it'll run south, and Ranulf, standing ready at the edge of the grove, will bring it down.'

Then he himself shot, with his special arrow—and missed. For once he had not bargained for a cross wind. Somewhere the arrow dropped from sight. The stag fled uphill to the south-east, terrified, but unhurt. But the King, with his special arrow, was more successful. Tirel saw the royal stag spring to the west, wounded, but not seriously, stung merely enough to swerve all the faster on the only route to safety, not to the north from which it had been driven, not to the south from which the arrow had sped, but directly westwards. It ran straight towards the sunset. 'The King will be blinded by the sun, he'll have to stand stock-still,' thought Tirel. 'He can't take aim. It's up to Ranulf now— *he* can see clearly enough.'

He took the second special arrow from his attendant. There was a sudden shout from the right—a cry of dismay. Only a few heartbeats later, it seemed, there was another shout, two voices raised in wild alarm. And both of his companions, attendant assigned to him by Gilbert, forester assigned to him by Ranulf, took to their heels and left him. He felt fear then, and thought it was terror. It was later that he knew that fear and terror were two quite different emotions.

Fear sent him running to the right, brought him stumbling towards the oak and the group of wildly excited men, shouting, gesticulating, but a thick-set, red-haired figure in a russet tunic was not there. Fear drove him on, into the midst of them, pushing between his two brothers-in-law who had come up from the other direction just before him, past Fitzhamon and William of Breteuil, to stare down at the foot of the oak tree where the King lay dead, an arrow in his heart, the dead hand clutching at part of the shaft where it protruded from his body. Fear left him with his wits still about him so that he could hear the King's attendant crying out that the arrow had struck the King in the breast, that the King had clutched at the shaft, fallen forward, breaking the arrow as he hit the ground, and dying without a sound.

The terror began when Ranulf, who had turned the King's body over on its back, asked, 'From which direction did the arrow come?' and then, straightening up, clutching something in his own living hand, cried, in bewilderment, and holding out the broken shaft, 'But this is one of the arrows given by the King to Walter.'

Terror took control when one by one the shocked faces turned towards him, and another expression took the place of shock. He managed to say, 'I did not kill the King,' and then, when the faces and watchful eyes did not alter, he said, even more vehemently, 'I *could* not have killed the King!' Still no changes of expression, still the intolerable silence, and he cried out, 'I was in a different part of the Forest—I did not even *see* him—I could not see him at all!'

But for all the impression he made, he might never have spoken. As the King's brother came up, Walter Tirel suddenly realised, with a dreadful clarity, that for the rest of his life—if he were permitted to live—he would continue to protest as passionately—and as vainly—against the accusation of regicide.

Gilbert de Clare obviously had decided that his brother-in-law should live, for when Ranulf, knife upraised, sprang at Tirel, murder in his face, shouting, 'I should kill you!' and Tirel merely stood like a dumb beast, Gilbert caught the Chief Hunter's arm, threw him back with violence, and shielded Tirel's body with his own.

Tirel could hear someone stammering in harsh-accented, uncertain Norman-French. It must be the forester who had been with the King. Frantically he strained his ears. Whatever had happened in this nightmare, his arrow could not have killed the King. Could they not see it? His arrow, to hit the King, must travel some forty yards—and then swerve at an angle and travel another fifty yards. Could not everyone see that? Could not everyone see that even if this impossibility had occurred, the arrow thus deflected would have so little force it could not kill a fly? 'But don't think, don't think!' he told himself. 'Pay attention to what the forester says.'

The King's shot had grazed his stag. The animal had sprung away to the westward, straight into the blinding light of the setting sun. (Yes, that was right.) The King had dropped his bow hand, had stood quite still shielding his eyes against the late evening glare to watch where the stag went. And then an arrow had come from the west and struck the King in his breast. He had died without a cry.

Fitzhamon, almost collapsing with grief and shock, leaning against the oak tree, head on arm, still kept his wits about him.

'You are sure the arrow came from the left?'

Yes, the man was sure—this was the very question the Chief Hunter had asked when he came running up on hearing the first cry of horror. And the Chief Hunter had said, 'Of course—that must be it—didn't you see a stag running south, an arrow fly at it—*but miss*? Missed the stag, *but not the King*?'

Fitzhamon was still, with an effort, managing to speak and think.

'Did *you* see the arrow miss the stag?'

The man had not. He had caught a glimpse of the stag that had been missed, but he, like the King, was staring into the sun, trying to see where their own stag ran.

'What does it matter?' came Ranulf's low, furious voice. 'We have proof enough of what happened. There were six special arrows. Let us check on them. The King had four. He shot one. His attendant still carries three. He made a gift of two. Where is the Lord of Poix's attendant?'

'Here, my lord.' ('So he's turned up again,' thought Tirel.)

'How many special arrows have you?'

'One now, my lord. The other was—shot at the stag running to the right.'

'And now I hold the shaft of it, and the point of it is lodged in the King's body,' said Ranulf.

Fitzhamon gave a great cry, and threw himself on his knees

24

beside the dead man. 'I told you not to come!' he shouted. 'I begged you not to come!'

Under cover of the fresh commotion, Gilbert began to talk rapidly to Tirel. 'You must get away. Get on your horse, make for the coast. I'll give you a guide, and a couple of men as escort. Don't make for Southampton, that may not be safe—make more for the west. But don't worry—we'll see to everything.'

Tirel found himself walking up the rising ground to the south, Gilbert on one side of him, Roger on the other, their attendants to the rear, a compact little group. At one point he wanted to stop, to stare back in the wild stupid hope that it had not happened after all, that the King would be standing there, shielding his eyes from the sun, and this time no arrow would come, no arrow *could* come from the left.

'I could *not* have killed him,' he said, halting. Gilbert gripped his arm, urged him on: 'It was your arrow,' he said. 'You saw it.'

Yes, he had seen it. That was the evidence against which there was no argument. He let them take him away without protest after that.

When they had been riding for half an hour Tirel was so dreadfully thirsty that, against all the objections of his companions, he insisted on halting beside a stream to drink. Almost he was tempted to lap like a dog, but he made himself cup his hands and drink not as a beast drinks. The sun was setting in a blaze of crimson, and the red light transformed the water. 'If anyone knew I had drunk here,' he thought with a hysterical giggle, 'he would say the King's murderer stopped to wash the blood from his hands.'

They had a bare hour and a half of daylight before them when the flight began. The guide nevertheless decided to take a short cut over moorland to the river Avon. At the ford stood a smithy —and at the sight of it Tirel drew rein. A few hours before another smith had brought special arrows to the King. In sudden passion he cried, 'One of those arrows may have killed the King, but it could not have come from my bow! I am going back! There can be a search for it, my own arrow, I'll find it where it fell to the ground—'

The others gathered round him, arguing furiously. It was as much as his life was worth—he was a foreigner, knowing nothing of English affairs; if Earl Gilbert, who knew a great deal, said his only chance was to get out of the country—and so on, at great length and vehemence.

They really need not have taken such pains. Little effort was needed to quell the last small futile flurry of rebellion on Tirel's part. Docilely he allowed them to take his rein and lead him over the ford that was ever after to bear his name. It was dusk now. They were still ten miles from Poole, it would be night before the port was reached, there would be no moon, and there was wild trackless country before them, part wood, part marsh, with yet another river to be forded. Better to turn south, keeping the winding Avon on their left and make for sanctuary at the new priory of Christchurch. So south over the grey, featureless countryside of dusk, and the priory, but no rest for Tirel that night, only vigil in the chapel, and incoherent prayers, and finally one prayer articulate enough, to be repeated again and again, 'Sweet Jesus, if it's Your will, I accept that other men will never believe in my innocence, but of Your mercy let me know *myself* to be guiltless of this thing.'

They set out again at first light and were at Poole by sunrise. Tirel was taken straight to his ship; dully he supposed that someone had journeyed on overnight to make the necessary arrangements. He asked who had done this, that he might thank him, but received no answer. He tried to thank those who had accompanied him, risking so much, as he put it, but received only what he thought were surly glances or looks of contempt. There was no mistaking the contempt.

With a fair breeze and sixteen hours of daylight, the ship easily made the seventy-mile crossing to the Cotentin coast. After this, hard riding, of which he remembered little, and flinging himself from his horse as if he were still pursued when he came to his own courtyard, and still, as if in flight, clattering

26

up the stairs to Alice's room. She sprang to her feet as he came stumbling in and stared wide-eyed at him. 'They say I killed the King,' he stammered, 'but I did not—*I could not!*' Then he collapsed at her feet.

He slept for nearly two days, deeply, it seemed, yet he knew when his wife left him, and awoke, calling for her. When this happened on the Tuesday they told him she had left him only because a messenger had come from her brother, asking after his own safety. Tirel told them to ask Alice to come to him, bringing the messenger with her. He must know what had happened since he left the Forest.

Much had.

The King's brother, Henry, was now King himself, proclaimed and crowned.

'But there was a treaty between the King and his elder brother Robert—should either die childless, the other would inherit—in any case, Robert's the elder son, by primogeniture alone—'

Henry had claimed the throne by porphyrogeniture—he had been born in the purple, after his father had been crowned King of England. Robert had been born in Normandy years before, was no more than the son of a duke.

'As was the dead King,' said Alice, more alert than her husband had ever seen her. Alice, had he known it, was sharpening her wits for the long struggle to defend his innocence. 'And how can it all have happened *so soon?*' she demanded.

It appeared that Henry and the leaders of the hunting party had hurried to Winchester on the evening of the King's death. Henry had seized the Treasury that night and claimed the throne. The following morning he had set out for Westminster and arrived there that same evening. On the following morning, Saturday, he had sent for the Bishop of London and produced a charter, promising to abolish all the injustices that had prevailed during his brother's reign. And on Sunday the Bishop of London (the Archbishop of Canterbury being in exile) had crowned him King.

Alice prompted the man with questions; Tirel said nothing. He felt as stupid yet remote as when he had first begun to recover from a bad bout of fever, as withdrawn from his wife and the messenger as if there were a thick veil between them. All that he said when the man came to an end was, 'Wait a little before you go for refreshment. I will send for the priest to write down all you say.'

Alice sent for the priest, and asked after her brothers. They were well, said the messenger. They had gone with the new King to Winchester, and then on to London.

And then Tirel asked a question, and loudly. 'What of his brother, the dead King? Did they leave him lying in the Forest?'

The messenger, despite himself looking shocked at the demand for such information from the King's killer, said that the King had been buried at Winchester on the Friday.

'Who took him there?'

'I heard he was carried on the cart of a charcoal-burner,' said the messenger, and then, as Alice cried out disbelievingly, he began quickly, 'They say all the other carts were needed for the baggage and furniture—' and then floundered into silence. After a moment he tried again. 'But very many poor people followed the cart through Winchester, grieving.'

'Only the poor people!' cried Alice.

The messenger was pleased to give her some reassurance. 'No, lady, the Chief Hunter rode behind the cart all the way from the hunting lodge, they told me.'

The priest was coming in through the door. 'Go with this good man and as you take your refreshment tell him all that you have told my lord and me,' said Alice. She turned to tell the priest what was needed. The messenger lingered for a moment beside Tirel. 'They say,' he said, in a low hurried voice, 'that all along the road the King's body dripped blood.'

Tirel sat with his hand to his head. Alice, after firmly closing the door behind priest and messenger, saw him, and ran across the room. 'You're ill,' she cried, flinging her arms about him.

'No! No!' he said. 'But your brother's man said this to me—'
and told her.

Her teeth chattered as she said, shaking, 'Was the King not
dead, then? *For a dead man doesn't bleed.*'

'He was dead,' said Tirel. 'I know he was dead, the arrow
was in his heart. I wouldn't have left if I'd thought him alive,
he would have listened to me—'

'Would they have left him, mortally wounded?'

'His brother would—if he were in so great a hurry to get to
Winchester. Fitzhamon wouldn't.'

'We have heard nothing of Fitzhamon.'

Neither spoke of her brothers. After a moment Alice said with
determination, 'Now you must eat, too.'

The priest came back with his record of the messenger's
news; the messenger himself had already gone.

'He was very earnest on one point,' continued the priest. 'He
had seen nothing of these things. He had not been in Winchester
or London—he was at Tunbridge when the Earl sent word to
him to cross to France.'

'There was no need for him to say that,' said Tirel. 'Any man
who had gone from the Forest to Winchester and then from
Winchester to London in so short a time would have little
strength for coming here so fast.'

But it was only when the priest read to him, slowly, the man's
account of what had happened since the King's death that,
hearing it for the second time, he realised what a frenzy of haste
there had been.

Henry had reached Winchester by nightfall. That had meant
a hard pound in gathering darkness along a road that, Tirel
himself knew, was dangerous enough by daylight and there had
been no moon that night. They must have started out in the
opposite direction within mere minutes of his own flight to the
west. Someone must have recovered his wits quickly.

They covered the twenty miles, reached Winchester, summoned the other members of the court and Council who had

not been members of the hunting party, and Henry had claimed Crown and Treasury—because he had been born after his father had been crowned King. (Well, he could have thought that up in the ninety minutes jolting through the gathering darkness. Or perhaps he had thought it up years before, in bitter silence when he saw one elder brother taking Normandy, the other England, and only a castle for himself.)

He had left Winchester for London early on the next morning. How in God's name had he and his counsellors managed to get through so much first—letters written, asserting his claim, arranging the baggage (including the Crown itself), remounts, escorting men-at-arms—the actual formal election by the council of the new King? And he could not leave before his brother's funeral. Even if he had been roused at dawn after only a few hours' sleep, it still seemed unbelievable that so much had been accomplished.

And on Saturday he had produced his charter. When in the devil had that been worked out? Had Henry brooded on that, too, in the past?

The priest had not yet finished speaking. 'There was one item of news that the man forgot to tell you, my lord. It's already said that the new King intends to marry the sister of the King of Scots, she being descended from the Saxon kings.'

Two sets of pictures began to form themselves in Tirel's mind, side by side: Henry one third of the way to Winchester while he himself drank thirstily from the pool the colour of blood, Henry almost within sight of the white cathedral while he, beside the smithy, protested he must go back and assert his innocence, Henry in the Treasury, flaming torches about him, while he had knelt in the dark chapel at Christchurch and begged God to show him his own innocence.

The King's body had been brought to Winchester in the charcoal-burner's cart at about the time that he was going on board ship.

And the blood had dripped all the way.

He could not have been alive.

They would not have left him mortally injured. Fitzhamon would not have left him mortally injured.

But, as Alice said, they had heard nothing of Fitzhamon. Ranulf had been there, escorting the body—Ranulf who had tried to kill him because he thought he had caused the King's death, was scarcely likely to ride calmly for twenty miles while before him the mortally injured King was jolted to death in a charcoal-burner's cart.

Yet the dead don't bleed.

Suddenly he recalled that the priest had some skill in healing.

'Father,' he said, 'a dead body cannot bleed, can it?'

And the priest replied calmly, 'Normally no, my lord, but surely you must know that it is commonly believed that the wounds of a murdered man bleed afresh in the presence of his murderer?' then withdrew, not realising that as God's agent he had proved to Tirel his own innocence.

He should have known from the start, of course. Only one man could have shot that arrow into the King's heart—the man standing at the corner of the grove south-west of the King. He was less than twenty yards from his target, and his target had stood there stock-still, shielding his eyes against the sun, watching, like all other men in that neighbourhood save one, the wounded stag running west. And the exception, unobserved, had coolly, safely—if one knew Ranulf at all, almost in a leisurely manner—drawn his bow, taken aim and killed the King. No need for fumbling at an unexpected chance; he had known it would come. It was late (because of the King's convenient illness which had prevented an earlier start), the beaters would have to close in quickly, more than one stag would be driven into the glade, hurried shots meant some would have to miss. And once Tirel missed, Ranulf's arrow could come flying within seconds from practically the same direction.

Tirel could hear Alice crying out, 'Oh, my dear heart, you're sick,' could feel her tears against his cheek. 'No!' he said. 'No! I'm not ill. But for God's sake, let me think.'

The King's attendant, also blinded by the light, also looking after the stag, would have seen neither Ranulf's movement, nor his, Tirel's, arrow falling harmlessly to the ground. But Ranulf would have seen that arrow, and with it his chance—marking mentally all the while where that special arrow had fallen, so that it might be retrieved later.

But the King himself had died with a special arrow in his heart.

It was easy, if one really considered it. Ranulf had brought in the scared-looking smith who had presented the six special arrows. The smith had made more than six arrows; the extra were already in Ranulf's possession.

Even Tirel had noticed, at the time, how Ranulf had led the King to give two of the arrows to his foreign guest—and even Tirel had noted, later, how Ranulf had been furious when he had tried to give him the arrows in the forest—and Ranulf, his blue eyes glittering with excitement, had said to Tirel's attendant, 'See that your master uses them!'

Ranulf attempting to kill Tirel—lest Tirel, gullible though he was, might have noticed something, might even be vehement enough in his protestations of innocence to arouse suspicions in the minds of more acute men.

Ranulf, the first on the scene of the murder, to ask the right questions from the terrified servant—'From which direction did the arrow come?'—and, picking up the arrow shaft, to make the first accusation against Tirel.

Ranulf, positioning the victim and the dupe very carefully. No need for hurried planning—he had arranged it all days in advance. Then the rain and business had brought frustration; Tirel remembered Ranulf's chafing, ill-temper, the ill-temper that had brought the sudden bellow of rage from the King. What had the King said? He could not remember precisely, but he knew it had indicated that there had been some past occasion when Ranulf had asked some favour, and it had been refused.

But would Ranulf kill the King for that reason alone?

32

Hardly. But hatred could make him the willing instrument of another.

Tirel could hear Alice sobbing, imploring him to speak to her. 'Not yet,' he said. 'I must think. Take my hand—there. Now let me think on.'

But of course Ranulf was not the only person who had no need of hurried planning. Henry's preparations had all been made well in advance.

The claim to the throne, the charter.

The very planning of the ride to London.

Robert was coming home, married. His bride brought a dowry so that he could redeem Normandy. There would be children of the marriage. No chance of Normandy now for Henry.

And the King guffawing, 'That's a game two can play!' The messenger sent off to Scotland—to be overtaken by a messenger from the new King carrying the self-same suggestion, marriage with the Scottish princess descended from the Saxon kings, so that England would unite behind her husband.

'Then, Henry being King, it is useless for me to protest my innocence,' thought Tirel.

He would always be known as a regicide.

He was never to learn that the plotters had, indeed, made some mistakes. They had been over-confident, and had not bargained with that inevitable part of the English summer, rain. So that on the very night of the King's death, in the Low Countries, Hugh, Abbot of Cluny, was to be told that the King's life was at an end, and on the same day—but before the actual shooting—one Peter de Melvis in Devonshire met a man carrying an arrow who said to him, 'With this your King was killed today.'

But Tirel did guess at this moment of revelation that the loyal Abbot Serlo had learned something of what had been intended, had sent warning by a trusted monk—and the monk, finding the King surrounded by the very men against whom that warning should be given, had dared only to send the message in so veiled a manner that the King had laughed at it.

33

Nor did Tirel ever learn two facts learned by his son Hugh, the one set down by Hugh as a very old man. That the *Anglo-Saxon Chronicle* had written shortly after the death, 'The King was killed by an arrow shot by one of his men'—'Which affirms my father's innocence,' wrote Hugh, '*he not being one of the King's men.*' And then, more than fifty years later, Gerald the Welshman, in *De Instructione Principum*, wrote boldly that the man who shot the King was Ranulf de Aquis. 'Yet who will believe it now?' wrote Walter Tirel's son.

Walter Tirel, within moments of grasping the truth, now cried out, 'Why did they choose *me*?' And again he knew. They must have a stranger, unconnected with Henry, an archer good enough to be invited by the King—and fool enough not to realise he was being fooled. He clung to his wife's hand and realised something he could never tell her—that he had been selected by her brothers to be the dupe. And then they had hustled him away from the Forest because flight in itself was the most convincing admission of guilt. The 'escort' had been provided, not for his protection, but to make sure that he did not change his mind, stand and protest his innocence, raise doubts—

The ship so providentially found had been prepared for him in advance—or for Gilbert and Roger themselves if the plot failed. 'I suppose,' thought Tirel, 'I should be grateful that even Gilbert could not stomach Ranulf cutting my throat.' And then, 'But I must never let my dear Alice know that her brothers have used me so.'

After the day of the hunt the Lord of Poix often dreamed of cats. But now all four had human faces.

2

The High Cost of Dying

(Paris, 1943 and earlier)

My dear,

Half an hour ago you stormed out saying, 'And you're not making much effort to stop me, are you!'

I could hear your voice, but, as God's my judge,

> (*a*) I didn't really see you go,
> (*b*) couldn't (never wouldn't—believe me)
>   lift a finger to prevent your going.

Because—well, I've surfaced mentally now, but find myself between the devil and the deep blue sea (you must forgive the mixture of metaphors). Either I let you think me capable of going berserk (your phrase) not only once, but twice, at two completely harmless remarks made by you—that you'd chosen your veil and head-dress and it meant a shorter hair-style, and that you'd made a fairly obvious choice as to where we should spend our honeymoon. Or I tell you something which could well make you decide against marrying a man who—

Well, a man who believes something very peculiar happened to him in December 1943.

No, not in the prisoner-of-war camp. The only danger there was being bored to death. The peculiar thing happened after I'd got out and was on the run.

The other three fellows made for the north and Sweden; my French was adequate enough for me to pose as a French factory worker conscripted for service in Germany, and I gradually made my way to the west, getting scruffier and more sodden all the time. It never seemed to stop raining.

I reached Paris at last, went to the address I'd been given, collapsed on to a truckle bed in an attic, and three hours later was on the run again—someone had given the game away, and I had ten minutes to get out.

It was a dull, rainy evening with a bitter wind from the north, a few days before Christmas. I was in a part of Paris I didn't know at all, at the most I had ten minutes' breathing space—but breathing was becoming increasingly difficult, because I was all in. My legs were like cotton wool, I couldn't remember when I'd last had a decent meal. Somehow I drove myself along those greasy wet streets, but I knew that once I fell I'd be down for good.

But when I did fall I somehow hauled myself up again. Because I'd fallen on the steps of a building that was obviously a church. If I could drag myself inside . . . I could. Pushing the heavy outer door open almost did for me, though.

There was a faint light inside, and people, two people. An old man and woman. They were putting the final touches to a life-size Christmas crib. I shuffled down towards them, feeling that even if they were well disposed towards escaped POWs, the very sight of me after weeks on the run would make her shriek. But she didn't. The pair of them, in fact, would have taken it as all part of the day's work if the ass tethered near the crib had turned out to be the kind that had startled Balaam.

One benefit the Gestapo achieved in occupied territory—it cut loquacity. In any conversation you got down to essentials immediately.

'I am English—escaped prisoner of war.'

'Are the swine close behind you, monsieur?'

'Too close for comfort.'

The old woman took the old-fashioned lantern used to light the crib and went ahead; her husband picked up an armful of straw and told me to do the same. As he stumped along, and I walked beside him, he said he would bring me

36

some food as soon as it was safe; I could only nod. All that I really wanted was sleep.

We came to what I took to be the churchwarden's pew. Nearby was a slab of stone set in the wall—some kind of memorial tablet, I thought at first, until I saw there was no inscription on it, and then when the old fellow began to tug at it, I realised it must close a vault of some kind. I think I must have given some sort of startled grunt, because he swivelled his head round and said reassuringly that there was a space of some twenty cubic metres behind the slab, and air-holes. After that I gave him what help I could, and it was easy enough to squeeze through the narrow opening we made. 'It will not be insupportable,' the old man murmured, 'although everything in the vault was disarranged when a new heating apparatus was installed.'

I said what I needed most was peace and quiet.

They handed in the straw and the lantern, cautioned me against setting the church on fire, promised to be back with food as soon as possible, the slab was put back in place, and I was left to my peace and quiet.

I was glad of the lantern. Whoever had been responsible for putting in the new heating system hadn't employed very tidy workmen, and rubbish was still piled in messy heaps. I stepped over them, and held up the lantern to view my domain. To my surprise there was a little stone staircase, very steep and dark. Thanking God again for the lantern, I went down the steps to the actual entrance of the vault. This was a semi-circular affair with an arched roof supported by two pillars. There was no sign of coffins, for which I was grateful, although my chief concern was to locate the air-holes. The first two I found had been blocked up at some time, and I began to panic, but then I found one which hadn't, so I relaxed and put the lantern down on the floor. This was as damp and greasy as the pavements outside; calling down fresh blessings on the old couple I went up to collect my straw, and made a bed for myself.

Was I nervous? Honestly, I don't think so. I was too tired to think clearly about anything much, and in any case I'd been so desperate that even the most macabre of shelters was welcome.

All that I felt, beside tiredness, was a little flicker of curiosity, strong enough to take me across, before I settled down, and take a look at some roughly carved inscriptions on the wall, but they were only a series of Christian names followed by early eighteenth-century dates, telling me little or nothing about my involuntary hosts.

It was at this point that I realised that I hadn't a single match upon me—and had no idea how much oil there was in the lantern. That gave me quite a jolt; tired as I was, I didn't welcome the idea of a siesta in a pitch-dark underground vault. Odd how the dimmest of lights can bolster up your courage.

Still, there was nothing I could do about it, so I put the lantern on the lowest step of the staircase, and lay down on the straw, pulling my sodden coat about me, thinking, not for the first time, that one of the smells I liked least was the smell of damp wool.

Still, I had my peace and quiet.

But not for long.

The dream began in such a way that I thought at first that I was coming into the vault again; I was climbing down below ground level, and there was an archway. But then I knew this was a quite different place; the dark archway was in front of a low door, a door sunk into the earth and hidden by a double grating, an odd door, like the entrance to some subterranean passage, very small, low and narrow.

Behind the door was a small paved courtyard. I had to go down some stone steps to reach it; I can remember thinking that I must have been used to them because although the place was gloomy enough I made no use of the wrought-iron hand-rails. To the left was what I knew to be a guard-room; before me was a large door, pierced by a smaller one about three and a half feet high and there, before a huge table and looking comfortable enough in a large armchair, sat some kind of official. He knew me and nodded; I went on beyond him into a room divided in two by enormous bars; it was used by some men who were doing some kind of book-keeping. They nodded to me as well.

I didn't look at any of these people with any curiosity; I was used to them; as I passed them I mentally labelled them gatekeeper, book-keeper and so on. And, if you can imagine it, they seemed to grow progressively less distinct as I moved forward until at last, although I knew there were people about me in this place, I scarcely saw them.

At the back of the room was a door opening into a passage. I went along it until, on the right, I came to two small rooms. One of them was very dark. There were people in both rooms, many people, and there was a smell I knew—the smell of fear.

But I had never known it so strong, even when we lay in a ditch being dive-bombed alongside a road in northern France in 1940.

I could smell the fear in the place, but I couldn't see any of the people. All that I could see clearly was a basket, covered with canvas. And the thought of what lay under that canvas turned my stomach. Yet I knew I had to go across and take basket and contents away—because what lay under the canvas was worth something, I'd get money for it. So I went across to take the basket away; I even lifted up the canvas to take a look inside to make a rough guess as to what I'd make out of the contents.

I'm sorry—I must have scared you unduly. There was no raw head and bloody bones inside the basket. Merely hair. Hair of different colours—gold, brown, auburn, black, grey. From the length and texture, women's hair. And I was going to take it away to sell it for wig-making.

Innocuous enough? Perhaps; but at the sight of that shorn hair, I woke up in that damned vault sticky with sweat on a December night.

To the smell of a smoking wick. The lantern had just gone out.

And in the darkness there was a voice. I found it was my own. I was addressing the darkness, defending my action in selling the hair. I needed the money. How could a man live on a thousand francs, especially in these days—and, let it not be forgotten, I had to supply my own equipment. And didn't I work hard enough? On my feet day and night, in all winds and weathers, with not a single day of rest—I was worn out. People might remember I wasn't as young as I used to be— I'd done forty-three years' good and faithful service, it wasn't surprising that I tired easily these days.

Although there was no doubt I was half crazed at the time, the 'forty-three years' brought me up with a jolt. Here I was, talking like a man old enough to be my father. But it was no good—after about ten minutes, shivering now in that pitch darkness, I was off again, worse than ever. 'Two carriages permanently on hire,' I complained, 'that's fifteen francs a day whether I use them or not, and sometimes I have to get extra ones. Then there's five francs for the drivers, and *they're* hard to get. And my assistants expect *pourboires* too—I know you allocated four to me, but with all the work I've been given to get through four isn't enough, I have to employ seven, even seven's not really sufficient. And they're difficult. They keep asking for more and more wages, and I have to pay what they want, free lodging too, so that means keeping up a big house. I can't go on dipping my hand in my pocket for all these extra expenses—'

'Oh, shut up!' I said to myself. In wartime we didn't hear so much about the cost of living and wage-claims, so at least the monologue came as something of a novelty, but what I couldn't stand was the self-pity.

Then, to my consternation, I found myself whimpering, 'I'm so *tired* of it all—so tired.'

'Shut up!' my real ego said.

'Straw, bran, nails, sacking—all those were put down in the account I sent in to you earlier.'

'Shut *up*!'

'The incidental expenses are dreadful. Ropes, webbing, baskets. A carpenter. I'm out of pocket all the time, I take no pleasure in the work, and I'm so tired—'

'Dear God,' I whispered, 'am I going mad?'

'But I don't rush things, even so, and I show my clients all attention. I have a good manner—that has been remarked upon. Really, of course, it's not surprising, I've always had a gentle, compassionate nature. Sometimes a lady, taking her place, sits facing the horses; whenever possible, I've persuaded her to sit with her back to them, it's always better that way. Of course, it depends if she's going on the journey alone.'

My brain apparently had been invaded by the proprietor of a fleet of hackney coaches with a side-line in the *toupée* trade.

And then I was dreaming of the girl.

What kind of a girl? Modern, I thought, at first. Fair hair cut short. Yet wearing an odd dress, a kind of red smock, mock-medieval. A modern girl in fancy dress? I thought afterwards she would have fitted in very well with the Pre-Raphaelites, the William Morris circle, she had that intense, would-be soulful look their women went in for. The loose dress would fit in too.

And my overworked, underpaid friend? No getting rid of him—he was there, all right. Still inside my brain, if you follow. There with the girl. We were driving along together, and it was a late summer evening. Whoever my self-pitying incubus was, he'd never met anyone like this girl before; she roused him even from gloomy thoughts of low wages and high prices. In fact he—I—could scarcely take his—my—eyes from her face. Not that she took much notice of me, for she was sightseeing, yes, *sightseeing*. She had said to me that she did not know Paris, and I realised she was taking advantage of this long ride to see the city. Not that there was really all that much to see—old, tall houses, for the most part, but we did pass one rather nice seventeenth-century building with a fine balcony, and further on there was a pretty fountain—the part of me that wasn't the exploited tradesman noted, 'nice specimen of the rococo'. The girl took a long look at that.

So she wasn't medieval, unless the Middle Ages and the seventeenth and eighteenth centuries were all jumbled together in the dream.

It was a long drive, close on an hour and a half.

We passed shops. They were all closed, but the girl turned her head to look at the signs hanging above them—the typical provincial sightseer.

Did I talk to her? Twice. The surface of the road was horrible, the jolting rougher than anything you can imagine, and she couldn't help herself much. So I said to her that if she leaned against the rail she wouldn't be so badly shaken.

The second time was towards the end of the drive. Again I knew that there were throngs of people about, yet could see only one thing clearly—this girl, just as in the other dream it had been the basket of hair. Now until this point I—*I*—had been convinced that this oddly dressed creature was a provincial sightseer, but suddenly it came to me that whatever she was doing, no matter how much she affected to feel nothing but curiosity, she was afraid. Her throat was dry with fear, had contracted so much she couldn't swallow. As I've said, she was an intense-looking girl, soulful, the martyr-Antigone type. Until that moment, I was convinced, she'd felt only exultation, but now she was unsure, afraid—and hideously lonely. Even my other self was touched. He leaned forward towards her and said, 'It's a long time, isn't it?' She managed to smile then, to shrug, keep up the pretence of indifference. *His* mood was one of glowing self-congratulation. 'Not a single insult or word of mockery has ever passed my lips; I have received much praise for my decorous manner and unchanging gravity.' But within seconds his thoughts were drawn back to that magnet of a topic—hair and wages.

I was still gabbling about it when old Pierre came back.

Fever, of course. Only to be expected. Starving, exhausted, soaked to the skin—I'd have been raving wherever I'd hidden.

But, I think, if I had hidden elsewhere, the dreams of my delirium would have been different.

And the dreams went on.

When a plane had picked me up and brought me back to England, they said that on my first night in hospital I kept sitting up trying to write letters on the top of the sheet: more pay demands, of course. But now there was another twist—apparently I kept apologising for the *appearance* of the letters I was writing, but justified myself by asking what else could they expect when I wrote fresh from work, or even *at* work—I couldn't keep clean at my job, no matter how I tried. I actually started belly-aching over the state of my hands, horny and calloused through what I called 'contact with the fastenings of the plank'. And then, quite suddenly, I started screaming. I was looking down at my hands and said that blood had got down under the nails. Then they used the hypodermic.

They cured me pretty well—to be honest, I told them they'd cured me because I didn't want to be shut up for the rest of my life as a psychiatric case. The real cure could only come through psychical and historical research in Paris, but an unimpeded programme of this kind was scarcely possible for a British officer at that period.

I was posted eventually for liaison work with the Free French in the weeks before the Normandy landings. And there I more or less laid the ghost of my respectable, much-put-upon friend.

There was an artillery major I became friendly with—a major in the Free French forces now, a Jesuit before the war. We got talking one evening about the war, and the previous war, and the war before that—the war before that for France, that is, 1870—and then on to the Paris Commune and anti-clericalism.

'Because some intellectuals are anti-clericals,' said my friend with some asperity, 'it does not necessarily follow that all anti-clericals are intellectual. Many of them have only one idea in their heads—that any stick is good enough to beat the Church with. Do you know, in Paris in the 1860s there was a famous case when a completely innocent priest was supposed to have kept various individuals walled up in the vault of his church?'

'There must have been *something* to give people such an idea,' I said.

'Oh, of course—a man had been accidentally shut in the church, forgotten, you know, and he swore that he heard groans —sheer hallucinations, of course—he agreed he'd dozed off.'

Here I rather lost the thread of what he was saying, being lost in uncomfortable recollection of what had happened when I myself had gone to sleep in a church. Again sheer hallucinations, of course, but—

'Then the whole affair took on a new lease of life in 1871,' continued the reverend major. 'Some of the vaults of the church were opened and—not on the whole surprisingly, one would think—bones were found in them. Bones of the curé's victims, the revolutionaries declared triumphantly; they actually laid a carpet outside the church, deposited the bones upon it, and had an exhibition, duly publicised by a newspaper article describing in detail the descent by the little stone staircase to the prison and burial place of the curé's victims, the entry between the pillars upholding the arch, the pathetic inscriptions on the rough-cast walls:

BARDOM, 1713
JEAN SERGE, 1714
VALENT

Though for these, of course, even the most villainous nineteenth-century priest couldn't be held responsible, could he? Then— What's the matter?'

'Which church was this?'

'The Church of St Laurent. Do you know it?'

'I think so,' I said. My hands, for all my efforts, began to shake. 'You said there were stories about it seventy odd years ago?'

'Based on the discovery of bones in a vault—to be found in any old church.'

'But a man fell asleep there and *heard* things?'

'All hallucinations.'

'He didn't sleep in the vault, did he?'

'My dear fellow, who but a madman would sleep in a vault?'

'An escaped prisoner of war might—with the Germans after him.'

'*You* did? And *you* heard something?'

I told him the story more or less as I have told it to you. He heard me out, then told me to wait a moment. He went out, and came back carrying a fairly large book.

As soon as he reappeared, I demanded, 'Were the bones in the vault ever identified?'

'It was known which family owned that vault for a century.'

'A *respectable* family no doubt—he kept stressing that.'

'Oh, yes, a respectable, well-established family business, one might say—except that they were civil servants.'

'Civil servants—with all the talk of nails and sacking—and where did the hair come in?'

'All those things had their place. Yes, civil servants, at first appointed and paid by the Crown, originally by the Sun-King himself. Their Revolutionary masters, however, didn't pay so well—take a look at this letter.'

I took the book, and read:

'Day and night on their feet, whatever the weather may be, and not a single day of rest—work that might well disable the most robust. Is it possible for a man to live on 1,000 francs, especially in these days?'

And:

'He had fulfilled its duties for forty-three years. The overwhelming work that it entails makes him wish to bring his services to an end.'

And:

'Baskets, bran, straw, nails, sacking, etc. These are enumerated in the account already presented—'

I looked at the heading of the document:

'Observations on the circumstances of the executioner in Paris.'

I looked at the title of the book at the top of the page: *The Guillotine and its Servants.*

The major said, 'The vault was that of the Sanson family—the hereditary executioners.'

'And the girl?' I asked after a moment.

'Charlotte Corday, I should imagine—in the traditional robe of the condemned murderess. The hair was that of the doomed women, cut off at the Conciergerie and sold by the executioner and his assistants—"small profits" of his trade. Have you ever heard of a writer called Mercier?'

I shook my head.

'He lived through the Revolution, and in 1795 he wrote *Nouveau Paris*. There was a chapter devoted to Sanson. *I should like extremely to know the working of his mind,* Mercier wrote, *and whether he regarded his terrible office in the light of a mere profession—*'

'An underpaid, overworked profession,' I said.

'*He can sleep, they say; as it is perfectly possible that his conscience was quite untroubled—*'

'He was sorry for the girl for a moment, but if he lost sleep it was because of his out-of-pocket expenses.'

But the Father—and for all his uniform, I thought of him only as a priest, now—went on reading, '*How does he sleep, this man to whom the last words and last glances of those doomed heads were given before he severed them?*' and answered himself, 'Not altogether dreamlessly, I think.'

And can you understand why I, who shared those dreams one night, cannot bear to think of you being taken by me to see the sights of Paris—first having had your hair cropped short?

15 April, 1946

The following two stories deal with the outbreak of war in 1914. Europe was divided into two rival alliances, feverishly increasing armies and armaments, Germany and Austria confronting Russia and France, with Britain as yet not openly committed to the second group.

In June 1914 the Archduke Franz Ferdinand, heir to the Austrian throne, was murdered at Sarajevo. Austria suspected, with some reason, that the murder had been instigated by a Serbian secret society, and wished to punish Serbia. But Serbia was a protégé of Russia, and from 1894 French governments had committed their country progressively to the Russian alliance, even though this policy had been steadily opposed by the Socialist leader Jaurès, who obstinately refused to accept Europe as divided into two armed camps. To Jaurès a German worker was as dear as a worker from his own France; a European war to him was unthinkable, a war between brothers.

And there were also men who tried to combat the obsession of the soldiers to mobilise and strike the enemy first, realising that this, as a previous German Chancellor, von Bülow, had put it, was committing suicide for fear of death.

3
Heretics
(France, 1908–1916)

I can never again hear the sound of church bells without a
sickness of the spirit. Do you know the motto of Schiller's
Song of the Bells?

'*Vivos voco, mortuos plango, fulgura frango* (I summon the
living, I mourn the dead, I break the furnaces).'

I suppose I should take consolation from the fact that the
pealing of bells is hardly likely to attempt vain competition
against the din of the 210-millimetre shells that is the background music of Verdun.

Yet although this eternal shrieking and clamour kills remem-
brance of all other sounds it cannot kill the memory of things
once seen—the sights, in particular, of my dear Languedoc. I
was thinking the other day of the Cirque de Navacelles in late
spring—asphodels and lilies among the grey rocks, white
may and arbutus, yellow saxifrage, and the scent of wild
thyme everywhere. I tried to recapture that smell of wild
thyme; it was quite a task, lying in the obscene mud about
Verdun, where even the stench of gas shells brings a kind
of relief.

I think it will be many years before any flowers grow in the
corpse-clogged mud about Verdun—if, indeed, this war ever
ends. Sometimes it seems more likely that we will go on killing
each other until the last Frenchman and German and Austrian
and Russian and Englishman are dead, we who should be
brothers. Here we are, neighbours, close neighbours—one
might even use that American term 'buddies'. We have so

much in common. We live and die worse than rats in underground holes we have dug for ourselves. I can recall an occasion before this madness began—an occasion when the frontier between France and Germany was less—well, let us say less untidy than this present frontier, littered as it is with human débris. A French mine-working to the west of the frontier ran alongside the German coalface to the east. In the German mine there was an explosion, men were cut off. What did the French miners do? They tunnelled through at the risk of their own lives, rescued their German buddies, brought them up to the light of day, embraced them, fêted them, swore eternal friendship. And a couple of months later the governments of France and Germany brought these same men up above ground, stuck rifles in their hands and told them to shoot each other down. That's what comes of working under different managements.

My name is Roger-Raymond de Trencavel. My family is one that has consistently backed the losing side. My most famous ancestor owned all the land between Albi and Carcassonne to Béziers, and then he backed the Albigensian heretics. Still, if his judgment was faulty, he couldn't have been such a bad fellow, my namesake, Roger-Raymond de Trencavel. When the oafish northern 'crusaders' came in 1209 to besiege Carcassonne after massacring the entire population of captured Béziers, Roger-Raymond, believing that as Viscount he had a duty to his people, gave himself up as hostage in return for the safety of the people of Carcassonne, and died in prison. They're not so soft-headed these days. Imagine—but one can't imagine —a member of the Government coming down from Paris in this Year of Grace, 1916, and saying to the Germans, 'Look, take me as hostage and let all these poor devils of Frenchmen drag themselves from their putrid shell holes and limp off to safety.' These, after all, are not the days of thirteenth-century barbarism.

After Roger-Raymond's *beau geste* his family, or at least my branch of it, not surprisingly fell on hard times. According to

49

temperament they lived lives of tranquil enjoyment or loathed monotony in our obscure little corner of Languedoc. There was little to gild an essentially dull existence; the whole family seemed to live in a penance stretching over the centuries for Roger-Raymond's defiance of the Church. The estate to which I was born consisted of a smallish house of little, dark-panelled rooms with a preponderance of straight-backed chairs, a sunny terrace, along which only I ever seemed to walk, a garden of gravelled paths between clumps of pinks and verbena, stocks and wallflowers, a vineyard, with peach and apricot bushes planted with the vines, a few beehives. To this the estates of Trencavel had dwindled. Within the small-windowed house, the scent of potpourri and beeswax fought an eternally losing rearguard action against the smell of dry rot.

Has misery—for it is the misery even more than the danger that contributes to the hell of Verdun—made me a little crazy, as it has made so many crazy here? To lie in poisoned twentieth-century mud and brood on thirteenth-century heretics . . . There's an odd link, though. Civilians—and those who operate to the rear—call the ordinary soldiers *poilus*—hairy *poilus*. But that's not the name used in the front lines. Here they're the *bonhommes*. And this was how the martyred Albigenses were known.

And so I think of the day when my father took me to Mont-Ségur, where the last heroic Albigensian stand was made, and broken. Below the fortress is what the local people call the 'field of the burned', the 'field of pyres' or the 'field of martyrs', where those of the defeated who still survived were given to the flames. But today it is peaceful enough; there is grass, and violets, flowers and grass sprung from those who died dreadfully at the hands of fellow men. In seven hundred years will there be grass and flowers springing from the dead of Verdun? I hope, but do not think so.

Thanks to the Inquisition, which put to the question those of its Albigensian enemies who fell into its hands, we know something of the belief in which my forebears died. We know, for example, that they believed neither in Hell nor in Purgatory; the Devil's domain is this world: I crouch in my shell hole and agree.

But there is one prayer of the *bonhommes* I cannot aspire to repeat: *Lord, have no pity on the flesh born of corruption, but rather on the spirit imprisoned within.*

But I wish I could. It would help one to hear the shriek of the 210-millimetre shells with greater fortitude.

What above all one must not do is remember that in our minds less than two years ago there was light and hope. If one starts thinking this, assuredly one will go mad, like the dogs they used to bring up to sniff out the wounded until the poor brutes went rabid under the shelling. But in dreams one remembers. And then one hears the church bells, and the great voice quoting Schiller.

I was educated at the Lycée d'Albi. And one evening, when I was sixteen, having a little time to kill before the appearance of the wagon of a friendly neighbour, which would take me part of the way home, I was strolling about in front of the Cathedral, staring up at it.

If you have never seen Albi Cathedral, it is quite impossible to convey to you its extraordinary colour. It is red—and never more so than on a sunny day under a clear blue sky. People quarrel violently about the exact degree of redness.

'You don't like the colour, then?' a voice said.

It was the most magnificent voice I had ever heard. I turned. The possessor of the voice was satisfyingly Jove-like in appearance—strong, gold-bearded, with a kind of joyous humour in his bright blue eyes. He recalled childish ideas of how kings in fairy tales should look.

'No,' I said, 'I don't.'

'The colour's wrong?'

'The whole building's no real right to be there.'

51

'Why not?'

'Think of the kind of man who rebuilt it: the Bishop, Bernard de Castenet—also Inquisitor for the district, who'd keep men in prison for five years without light or air awaiting sentences. The Pope at Avignon selling indulgences wholesale—'

'A young Huguenot?' he asked, smiling.

'Oh, no!' Suddenly I felt foolish, and lapsed into silence.

'What's your name?' he asked gently.

'Roger-Raymond de Trencavel.'

'Ah, that explains much. Your appearance, if I may say so, is in accordance with the name.'

'The face of a loser?'

'Oh, no,' he said. 'Rather let's put it like this—the face of one prepared to lose much if the cause is good.'

Our neighbour appeared at the far end of the square, halted abruptly, beckoned sharply.

'I must be late,' I said. 'Your pardon, monsieur—I must go quickly.'

I hurried across to our neighbour. He was frowning angrily. 'What in the devil do you think you're doing, my boy, talking to that fellow?' he demanded.

'Fellow, monsieur?'

'Yes, that damned mountebank of a demagogue, Jaurès.'

After a moment, he said, 'Obviously you had no idea who he was. In the circumstances I shall not inform your father, and shall consider the incident as forgotten.'

Our neighbour, I should explain, held shares in the Carmaux Mining Company. He had, therefore, hated Jaurès steadily for sixteen years.

Carmaux was a district with a long record of bitter labour disputes. In 1892, the year I was born, the secretary of the miners' union, a Socialist, had been elected Mayor. He was dismissed by the Company when, having been refused leave of absence for his duties, he took it anyhow. The miners had struck in protest. The owner of Carmaux owned not only iron mines; he owned glass works, timber forests, he had a seat in the Chamber of Deputies. The David who took on this Goliath of a magnate was the thirty-three year old Jean Jaurès, a professor of philosophy at Toulouse, like myself educated at the Lycée d'Albi.

Our neighbour, of course, had not looked on the situation as that of David and Goliath; he saw it as a re-enactment of an earlier episode, when Satan had stirred up discontent in Heaven itself.

At school next day I tried to find out more about the bearded man with the splendid voice. This was easy enough—he was the school's star pupil, who'd gone on, moreover, to be the star pupil of the Ecole Normale, the youngest Deputy when he had been elected at the age of twenty-six. Then he had become disillusioned with politics, had returned to academic life as Professor of Philosophy at the University of Toulouse.

A week or so later my father went to Toulouse, to visit his bookseller. Our peaches were excellent that year—you felt you could almost blow the skin off them—so there was a little extra money. I begged leave to go with him. The bookshop was just off the Place du Capitole. From it a narrow street, the Rue du Taur, runs towards the University quarter. Leaving my father safely immersed, centuries away, in the bookshop, I hurried off. I didn't like to ask the students, or anyone who looked professorial, but I summoned up the courage to ask some kind of clerk, coming out of an office marked 'Enquiries', 'Do you remember when Professor Jaurès lectured here?' and he pushed past me, snapping, 'How can I forget it? He ruined the tone of the University! Townsfolk—even workmen, *artisans* crowding in to hear him—scarcely any room for students and his colleagues! It created much bad feeling, I can tell you!'

I went back to the bookshop. Father was haggling over a copy of Schmidt's *Histoire des Cathares et Albigeois*; I withdrew to the portion of the shop which had shelves of reference

53

books, warily took one down. 'In 1893, Jaurès re-entered the Chamber of Deputies as member for Carmaux, having stood as a candidate for the French Workers' Party—'

That was the year our neighbour remembered with a shudder over many a glass of wine, '93, when the Socialists, with half a million votes, sent thirty-seven Deputies to the Chamber. To hear our neighbour talk, you would think he was alluding to the '93 of the previous century, when the Terror was filling the tumbrils daily.

Toulouse was full of quick-tempered voices that day. 'When you've finished—' came staccato from beside me. An angry little man with gold-rimmed pince-nez, who seemed angrier still when, staring down at my betraying index-finger, he saw what I had been reading. 'So!' he said, with no appearance of pleasure. 'Another young fool's fallen under the wand of the enchanter . . . No!' he continued, though I had no intention of replying, 'don't deny it! Above all, don't excuse yourself! Haven't I seen even those who detest his politics queue to hear him speak because, they say, his phrasing's so admirable! Well, why can't they be content with listening to a good actor declaiming Racine? Students come to my classes for instruction, pure instruction, thank God!' He snatched the reference book away from me, and I beat a hasty retreat.

I think my obsession with this man encountered once, and then briefly, was understandable enough in a boy of sixteen who returned each day to a house that sometimes seemed as stilled as the interior of a pyramid-tomb, my mother at her embroidery frame, or reading some religious work or other, offering a pale, cold cheek for my kiss at the end of the day, but never an embrace, my father shut up in his study, brooding on the remote past, his family's swift descent from greatness in the thirteenth century (but never much thought of the slow decline since). He saw the events of 1209 in a strictly personal sense; to me one of the chief tragedies of the Albigensian War was that it brought to an end a free land, where people could be *happy*; at first my interest in Jaurès was kept in check by the thought that he was, after all, a Socialist—was his Socialism Marxist Socialism? That, so far as I understood it, didn't mean freedom. But then, with enormous relief, I read that he had said that future Socialist society would be unacceptable if it did not allow men to 'walk and sing and meditate under the sky'.

It is something to cling on to, that thought—that at some time in the future men will be able to walk and sing and meditate under the sky.

At eighteen I was at the Sorbonne. Mother at first detested the idea; eventually it was arranged that I should stay at the home of her widowed second cousin, Cousin Amélie, in the Rue de la Bienfaisance.

'You will call,' my mother had said, 'on these friends and cousins when you are in Paris. And be sure you do it in the correct manner.' She had further depleted our shaky finances by having visiting cards printed for me, had purchased several new pairs of gloves for me—the gloves were very important. Poor mother. When I paid the call *I'd* always had in mind, to the apartment in Passy, at the Passage de la Tour, I showed all the finesse of a young bull blundering into a china shop.

I was admitted by an elderly woman wearing a red wrapper. In one hand she held a duster. Certainly this was the home of Monsieur Jaurès; was he expecting me to call? No, I said, but—well, I was from Albi. 'Ah,' she said, 'then I've no doubt he'll see you. Will you wait here while I go upstairs?'

She took me from the rather shabby hall with its zinc umbrella stand into the drawing-room. Nothing could have been more respectable—wax flowers, family photographs in plush frames, a girl's first communion wreath, fading. (I was to learn that letting his wife send their daughter to her first communion meant defying most of the party.) In sudden agonies of embarrassment I realised, from the family photographs, that it must be Madame Jaurès who had had to interrupt her dusting to admit me. She came back; yes, her husband would see me. We went out into the hall. Hanging near the umbrella stand was a frock-coat, its pockets torn. To my dismay, Madame Jaurès caught me glancing at the garment. She shook her head. 'He's always stuffing papers, pamphlets in his pockets, ever since I married him. So the pockets become torn and shapeless, and I can do nothing about it!'

We climbed the stairs and into a room lined with shelves laden with books, pamphlets, papers—like my father's study, but while that was like a mausoleum, this was like a power house, with a human dynamo sitting shirt-sleeved at a trestle-table, writing furiously.

'You've finished your coffee,' said Madame Jaurès. 'I'll bring you another pot, and a cup for the young gentleman.'

'Of course, my dear, of course.' The door closed behind her. 'Now, young man, sit down. Do I know you?'

I faltered, 'I'm here under false pretences. We spoke once, briefly, two years ago, outside the Cathedral in Albi—'

'Wait a moment, I remember it; give me another moment, and I'll remember your name. One of the nobles—no, not Raymond of Toulouse, it was one of the better men—of course, Roger-Raymond de Trencavel, the face fits the name even better now.'

Madame Jaurès came back with the filled coffee-pot and the extra cup. 'My dear, our young visitor isn't only *from* Albi, his people *were* Albi once—he's a de Trencavel, imagine it. Now, young man, draw your chair closer and tell me what I can do for you.'

I honestly don't know what I told him; perhaps it's just as well for shame's sake that I can't remember what I said. I can't even remember what was said in reply, but we finished the coffee-pot between us, and I finally came away from the Passage de la Tour with the knowledge that my host rose at half-past six every morning, and went for an hour's walk, and that I would be welcome to join him on any or all of these morning rambles.

And so my real education began.

56

The talk could be of anything. One day it was on *Don Quixote*—Jaurès had learned Spanish in order to read it. Or it could be how the Tarn ran red after heavy rains because of the detritus in it, or the Romance of Renaud of Montauban. But, for weeks, nothing of politics. Finally, one morning in late autumn, with our feet rustling through drifts of tawny fallen leaves, I hesitantly brought up the subject of Socialism. He turned and looked at me. 'Well, my dear fellow, what's your definition of Socialism?'

'I read the other day—' I began.

'Read! That's not the way to come to Socialism! That's the way Marx did things—sat (when he didn't have boils on his behind) for years in the Reading Room at the British Museum, seeing through other men's eyes the conditions of the poor! So many of these damned desiccated so-called Socialists think Socialism began with Marx. It didn't. It's the product of end-less, timeless suffering. And that you must see for yourself.'

'Will you take me?'

'Yes. We'll start tomorrow.'

He took me into the slums of Paris. Hunger, dirt, stench— the stench of stale urine, rancid cooking-oil, latrines—and noise. Babies wailing, men cursing, shouting obscenities, women screaming, consumptives coughing on to bloodspotted bits of rag. Women in childbirth on filthy straw, old people dying on filthy straw, and death the only escape from drink, prostitution, crime, misery, endless toil.

'And don't think this happens only in Paris!' Jaurès said to me. 'It's happening all over the world.' He translated to me part of a book by Jack London, *People of the Abyss*. There had been a young man, not much older than I, with a sick mother. He lost his job, and tried to drown himself, failed, and was charged with attempted suicide. The lock-keeper's wife pulled the puny wretch out of the river, but 'as fast as I pulled to get him out, he crawled back,' until some workmen came to help her. The magistrate congratulated her on her muscular strength and the court laughed, but London wrote, 'All I could see was a boy on the threshold of life, passionately crawling to a muddy death.'

'Never forget,' repeated Jaurès, 'that this misery is happening everywhere.'

'Never forget,' he said to me on another occasion, 'that man is good, and that, because of this, all society can be made good, but it will mean a struggle, a struggle to be fought daily. But it's not *guerre à l'outrance*; we're not the wolf at the door waiting to devour the better-off, our job is to make the better-off realise the importance of the workers, so that the better-off themselves will become our allies.'

So, from a family that lived bitterly in the past, I came to know this man who thought hopefully only of the future. 'Do you know how to spot an article by Jaurès?' another politician asked once. 'Very simple; all the verbs are in the future tense.'

Jaurès had, however, one fear for the future. War. The culmination of the fratricide that began when Cain struck down Abel—'Yet worse again. Cain struck down Abel because he wanted to kill his brother; nowadays men kill their brothers at the orders of men sitting in comfort and safety—padded armchairs behind closed doors, Gobelins on the wall, Aubussons on the floor—that's how the conspiracy's carried out nowadays!'

In particular he hated and feared the alliance between France and Russia. 'It's an instrument of war—particularly since that swine Isvolsky came to Paris as Ambassador.'

Isvolsky, the Russian Ambassador in Paris, had previously been his country's Foreign Minister. In 1908 he had tried to bring off a sensational *coup*, the opening up of the Straits, the Dardanelles, to Russian warships. He had visited the Austrian Foreign Minister, Aerenthal, and had promised that if Austria did not stand in Russia's way in this matter, Russia would make no protest if Austria annexed outright the Turkish provinces of Bosnia and Herzegovina, which she already administered. So Austria took the provinces, but Russia failed to achieve the opening up of the Straits.

He was a mass of conceit, Isvolsky. One saw it in his appearance. He was a short, plump man, who strutted, never walked. His clothes, tailored in England, were nevertheless—and no doubt on his instructions—a shade too tight. Always a pearl tie pin, a monocle, white spats, patent leather shoes. His hair, carefully parted, also seemed to be manufactured from patent leather. A carefully waxed moustache, a pasty face. An odd way of talking—a kind of carefully cultivated rasp. 'It is his method of trying to impress upon you that he is a great Russian noble, what they call a *barin*,' said Jaurès. Unfortunately for Isvolsky, this was not the impression he did leave; one remembered plumpness, pastiness, artificiality, his habit of never looking at you directly, always turning away with a sidelong glance—and the smell of Parma violets. One has to be careful with that particular scent. So often it can smell cheap and cloying.

But Isvolsky's physical vanity was as nothing compared with his intellectual conceit. His scheme had failed. Britain would not give consent, and he had little support in Paris. But he could not admit he had miscalculated. Austria had tricked him. 'The dirty Jew's swindled me,' he said. (The Austrian Foreign Minister reputedly was part-Jewish.) And Germany had stood by her Austrian ally.

From that moment Isvolsky was obsessed with the idea of revenge. Only the destruction of Austria and Germany could provide the salve for his smarting vanity. But Russia could not fight Austria and Germany single-handed; Isvolsky had come to Paris as Russian Ambassador and thrown himself into his self-imposed task as incendiary with such success that at a dinner party in August 1914, he was able to announce proudly, 'This is my war!'

To be fair, he alone was not wholly responsible for the corruption and entanglement of France. From 1905 the Russian government had been systematically buying the French Press, *Le Temps*, *Le Matin*—almost every newspaper. (Except, of course, obvious exceptions like Jaurès' *L'Humanité*.) So one had the *Echo de Paris* telling its readers that 'War is truly regenerative.'

But until the beginning of 1913, even Isvolsky's undying malice could not get the results he wanted. In January, however, a new President was elected in France, Poincaré, a Lorrainer, of whom his predecessor said, 'I greatly fear that war is entering the Elysée after me.' 'No,' said Jaurès when he heard this, 'let's be fair. Poincaré would deny he's a warmonger. But, he would say, he's a realist, and since war's inevitable (remember he's a Lorrainer, and war's the only way of getting Lorraine back from Germany) we must be prepared. In the process, he's going to dig a ditch between the nations he thinks can help him and those he knows will oppose him. We must fling bridges across that ditch!'

Jaurès' great hope lay in that brotherhood of nations that he preached with such unswerving faith. For that reason he had drafted the declaration passed at the Internationalist Socialist Congress in Stuttgart in 1907, passed again three years later in Copenhagen:

'If war threatens to break out, it is the duty of the working class in the countries concerned . . . to use every effort to prevent war by all the means which seem to them most appropriate . . . Should war nevertheless break out, their duty is to intervene to bring it promptly to an end . . .'

Inevitably, of course, someone known to Cousin Amélie found out I was often seen in Jaurès' company, and told her. A painful interview followed. I discovered that my early-morning exits had been interpreted as religious fervour; I had been stealing out to Mass. 'And I told Father Etienne, I was so proud of you! He said I must be mistaken, and he was right—so right! As for your mother's grief—what can I say? And your father—when he hears of this, he'll cut off your allowance, order you home!'

I said in consternation that I had honestly never tried to deceive her into believing I was creeping off to early Mass.

That gave her a new idea. Poor soul, she dreaded breaking the terrible news to my parents, who might accuse her of negligence in guardianship. So first she would consult her confessor. 'You must talk to him too. I'll ask him to tea tomorrow.'

So there was tea—biscuits and cherry jam—and Cousin Amélie in her Nattier-blue dress with the lace collar, tremulously consulting Father Etienne. 'Roger has been talking to Jaurès!' But, to her amazement, Father Etienne was not unduly shocked. 'He won't corrupt the boy, madame. He has a good mind and a fair mind. For example, he's written a so-called "Socialist" history of the Revolution which in fact is remarkably impartial! And he is honest, completely honest.'

'He's always quoting to me, "I am resolved to speak whatsoever I dare do, and am displeased with thoughts not to be published," ' I said eagerly—also artfully, for in previous conversations I had learned the Father was a great admirer of Montaigne.

He finished the quotation now. ' "The worst of my actions and conditions seem not so ugly unto me as I find it both ugly and base not to dare to avouch them." Well, I can't think of a much better motto.' Then, after a meaning look at me, he turned solemn eyes on his parishioner. 'You know,' he said, 'he doesn't rush around the streets with a smoking bomb in each hand, madame! He goes to garden parties at the British Embassy and actually went to the Elysée Palace in 1903 to attend a banquet given in honour of the King and Queen of Italy.'

'Italy!' said my cousin. 'The so-called king who's robbed the Holy Father of—'

'Yes, yes,' said Father Etienne hurriedly, 'but garden parties at the British Embassy! What could be more respectable?'

There was a moment's silence. Then Cousin Amélie announced, 'I shall invite him to dinner and see him for myself. You will come too, Father.'

She was not intrepid enough to face Anti-Christ alone. A few hours later she was telling me she would invite some of what she called her 'worldlier' acquaintances, too—presumably to draw the fire lest Anti-Christ aimed his guns devastatingly at her and Father Etienne, unsuccoured.

So there came the evening of the dinner party, Cousin Amélie quaking, Father Etienne interested, the other guests superciliously expectant. So one might await the arrival of a tiger in a cage, to go through a few simple tricks—after one had been assured his claws had been clipped!

And Jaurès came, saw, and conquered. They expected a fanatic, they met a man filled with the joy of life, with good-will to all, a Viking in looks with the tongue of an angel. We sat there on Cousin Amélie's Directoire chairs, in her blue-green dining-room, and Jaurès talked—as he always talked, quite unaffectedly—and his fellow guests, unused to such talk, sat spellbound. Cousin Amélie forgot to rise and lead off the ladies, the men forgot their need for brandy and cigars, the very servants, having removed the dishes, came back and stood at the door of the room, listening.

I remember how next morning he threw back his head delightedly when I told him that Cousin Amélie's supersilly niece Hortense had said, before leaving, 'Do you know, Auntie, I *knew* my nose was shining, but I *couldn't* tear myself away to go and powder it!'

In 1912 it seemed as if catastrophe were very close. There was war in the Balkans, where Russian interests clashed with those of Austria. An emergency Socialist conference was summoned to be held in Basle, this being on the Swiss frontier between France and Germany. Any lingering doubts Cousin Amélie may have possessed were dispelled by the news that the Church authorities had given over the Cathedral to the conference despite protests of 'dangerous consequences'. In fact, she insisted on paying my fare. She could remember the war of 1870 all too clearly.

Five hundred and fifty-five delegates, drawn from twenty-three countries, turned up at Basle, unanimously approved a manifesto proclaiming 'readiness for any sacrifice' against war.

And Jaurès spoke from the pulpit of the Cathedral.

'The sound of the church bells reminds me of the motto of Schiller's *Song of the Bells*: *Vivos voco, mortuos plango, fulgura frango*. I summon the living, I mourn the dead, I break the furnaces.' He bent forward. 'Now I call on the living that they may defend themselves from the monster who appears on the horizon. I weep for the countless dead now rotting in the East. I will break the thunderbolts of war which menace from the skies.'

War was averted in this autumn of 1912, but in the following January Poincaré was in the Elysée Palace and two months later France enlarged her army, increasing the period of military service from two to three years. This was on Russian insistence. In the Chamber Jaurès denounced the measure as a crime against the Republic, outside the Chamber he addressed a crowd of 150,000 at an open-air meeting. 'Pacifist! Pro-German!' screamed most of the Press—the Press subsidised by Russia.

I graduated, began to work on the paper founded and edited by Jaurès, given by him, characteristically, the title *L'Humanité*. Mother had hysterics, Father emerged from the thirteenth century long enough to cut off my allowance and cut me out of his will; Cousin Amélie, won over by Viking grandeur and the knowledge of that first communion wreath, wrote valiantly to Albi that, 'Roger knows that there will always be a home here for him with me.'

The summer of 1914. Poincaré was going on a State visit to Russia. In the Chamber Jaurès refused to vote for the credits for the trip; it was dangerous for France to become increasingly enmeshed in Balkan adventures, and in treaty commitments of which the French people knew nothing. At the end of June news came that the heir to the Austrian throne had been assassinated by a student in an obscure capital of an obscure province—Sarajevo. More headlines were given to the result of the Grand Prix de Paris, run on the same day.

Baron Maurice de Rothschild's Sardanapale, the favourite, had won at odds of eighteen to five.

Poincaré left for Russia.

Isvolsky (the most dangerous man in Europe, Jaurès was now calling him) would also return to Russia at the same time.

The next great international Socialist conference was due in August, in Vienna. But then came news of the Austrian ultimatum to Serbia—to wait until August to make any peace demonstration might be too late. A meeting of Socialist leaders was summoned to Brussels for July 29. In the days before we left, the messages flooded in to *L'Humanité*'s office—'We are all relying on you, Jaurès, to stop the war.' They came from all over Europe.

The train seemed to crawl on its way to Brussels. We passed through dreary industrial districts. There had been some uneasy talk of what Poincaré, who had still not returned from Russia, had promised and extorted at St Petersburg. Jaurès had been staring out at acre after acre of industrial waste. Suddenly he said, 'He wants war, and he's a Lorrainer! In Lorraine the mines run along the frontier as they do here, the shafts run so close that the German miner at times hears the pick of his French comrade, crawling in the dark like himself. Will *they* come up above ground to shoot each other down?'

It was raining when we reached Brussels, one of the few days in that summer when the weather was not brilliant. The Belgian Labour movement had just built for itself a fine new building, the Maison du Peuple; the delegates met here in a small hall. Moods matched the weather. Most delegates seemed to be hoping for a miracle to happen. There was talk all day; all that came out of it at the end was that discussions were to be resumed on August 9, in Paris.

But that evening a mass meeting was held at the Cirque Royale, and the Belgian workers came to it. They came from all parts of the city and suburbs, they left their benches, their lathes, their engines, they brought their wives and their children up from the stinking airless tenements, the narrow streets of nightmare I had come to know so well, they came pale-faced, shabby, tired yet excited, to see one man.

He stood on the platform with his arm about the German Haase's shoulders—let this gesture deny any enmity between the French and the German people!

In that stiflingly hot arena, hope began to revive a little.

When he rose to speak the clamour was so great that for minutes he could not make himself heard. I have known men denied the right to speak because there were those in the audience who hated them; I have never known men prevented so long from speaking—because of love.

And because I was absorbed in this thought I didn't hear all that he said. That is possible, you know. You can pay the deepest attention to a person—and not hear what he says. But I heard enough. He praised the noble German Socialists who had shouted '*Nieder mit dem Kriege*' as they marched down the Unter den Linden. If Russia were to march tomorrow, the French workmen would say, 'We know no secret treaty, only the public treaty with humanity and civilisation.' But there was not a moment to be lost. Attila stood at the very brink of the abyss. His horses' hooves trampled the grass of the battlefield. But he, Jaurès, swore to his German comrades that the French 'will continue to support them like brothers against the warmongers' Attila campaign, true till death.'

The audience rose to him with thunderous cheering. I do not know whether he planned to end his speech there, or whether the storm of applause cut him short. But the last word he spoke in public was 'death'.

But he was all life, all quivering, eager, intense life as he stood there, and the crowd rose to him, then poured into the street, formed a parade, shouting '*Guerre à la guerre!*' and the Germans and Austrians called, in their own language, the same thing, '*Nieder mit dem Kriege!*'

Next day we returned to France. Jaurès, walking across the Place du Sablon with the Belgian Vandervelde, was confident.

65

'My old friend, there'll be ups and downs, no doubt, but it's impossible that the affair can't be settled. I've a few hours before my train. Let's go to the Museum and see the Flemish primitives.'

But Vandervelde was leaving for London, so we had to go to the Museum without him. The paintings affected Jaurès greatly. He was still deeply concerned about the results of Poincaré's visit to Russia. 'I planned to go there once,' he said. 'I read up all I could about it. There was an English guide—Murray's—published about half a century ago which had a description of St Petersburg I've never forgotten—"St Petersburg floats like a bark overladen with precious goods while the waves seem as if, deriding her false foundations, they could overturn in a few hours that which the will of man had raised with such untiring labour." That's European civilisation for you—such frail foundations, such vulnerable materials, so precious a load in so fragile and faulty a vessel. I'm European. I love my Languedoc as much as any other man from the Midi, I'm as good a Frenchman as any other born in *la patrie*, but I'm also a European. And there aren't enough of us. We're a minority, a sect. We must gain the time to convert others, and here we are threatened by this frightful war!'

In the train he brooded over the manifesto he had written the previous evening, fresh from the speeches, the applause, the peace demonstration. 'The Socialist Party proclaims aloud that only France can dispose of France's fate; that in no circumstances must she be involved, through the more or less arbitrary exploitation of secret treaties and unknown obligations, in a frightful conflict—'

Poincaré would be back in Paris before we arrived.

We crossed the frontier. Jaurès stood looking out of the window, back to the east, to Belgium—and Germany. 'I told Haase to work on the Austrians,' he said. '*His* is the dangerous task. He may fail.' And then, suddenly, still looking eastwards, he began to quote from the *Aeneid*—'O, ashes of Troy, and

66

you, shades of my companions, I take you as witnesses that in your disaster I recoiled neither before the shafts of the enemy nor before any kind of danger, and that, if my destiny had willed it so, I should have been worthy to die at your side.'

Jean Longuet, one of those travelling with us, said, 'That's less apt than your quotations usually are.'

'And more pessimistic,' I said.

'Is it? I suppose so. But then I'm tired. I'll snatch a little sleep while I can.'

We were all tired, but he alone was successful in achieving deep sleep. The rest of us drowsed fitfully, jerked back to sudden wakefulness, felt the heat of the sun beating on the windows of the compartment. After one such unrefreshing doze, I awoke with a start, frightened like a child by some formless nightmare, stared, as a child will look to a parent for reassurance after that nightmare, across at the face of the man who in my thoughts had been my father for four years now.

He was still deeply asleep. Indeed, it seemed something deeper than sleep. I touched his hand; it was warm. Beside me I heard Jean Longuet catching his breath. 'Did you have that feeling too?' he whispered. 'I was suddenly overpowered with the thought that he was—dead.'

Jaurès awoke when we arrived in Paris, sprang into immediate action, tried to brush the creases from his shabby frock-coat, smoothe down the ruffled golden hair now streaked with grey.

'Ready for action!' he said.

The train steamed into the Gare du Nord. There was a great crowd waiting, chanting 'Jaurès! Jaurès!' as if it were an incantation. They were terrified; only he could inspire them with some of his own courage—

'It all depends on him,' Longuet murmured to me, but Jaurès heard, swung round.

'No! It all depends on the German comrades!'

Seconds later we realised we could not be sure that the

Germans would stand firm much longer. We were surrounded by set-faced men. 'Russia's mobilising! You know what that means!'

He said, quite steadily, 'Yes. This—this demon-bogey of Tartar invasion may make Socialists in Germany react *as Germans*, deaf to all but the idiot cries, "Get our blow in first!" Well, we're up against it, my friends.' He squared his shoulders. 'Just as well I took that nap in the train.'

'Jaurès! Jaurès!' shouted the crowd.

Now he was more essential than ever. Only he could hearten the German Socialists to stand firm against war-planning from above, war-fever from below.

'Is Poincaré back?' he asked.

Yes, he had returned the previous day to this same Gare du Nord. 'You've just missed seeing the last of the flags being taken down. It was like the return of a triumphant Caesar—flowers, flags, singing. Gold braid everywhere, but he made straight for Isvolsky, who'd got back earlier.'

Jaurès made up his mind. 'I'll go straight to the Foreign Ministry. If Russia's turned mad dog there's still a hope we can restrain her.'

We drove to the Quai d'Orsay. I strolled about waiting as he went inside. It had been another glorious day, and many people, already on holiday, had taken advantage of the weather and gone out into the country. There were still a few slanting rays of sunlight in the streets, and suddenly, from the direction of the Gare d'Orsay, the holiday crowds came pouring along the road, chattering, laughing, singing, joyous life itself, arms full of fragrant blossom, fathers carrying drowsy children, lovers with arms entwined. My spirits lifted. Here was a foretaste of the society of the future, where free men could walk and sing and meditate. I turned back, and there was Jaurès. He was bitterly depressed; no one would listen to his pleas that France should put pressure on Russia to cancel or at least postpone her mobilisation. I tried to tell him of the joyous crowds, but he suddenly stiffened, then pointed. Approaching the door of the Ministry was a plump, strutting figure. 'That scum Isvolsky is getting his war!' said Jaurès.

Isvolsky heard him. Ludicrously, his monocle fell from his eye. I laughed, I could not help it. The Russian looked at me like a cat, eyes narrowing, tongue passing over lips. I stopped laughing. He was not ludicrous, he was sinister. The odour of Parma violets might as well have been the stench of the charnel-house.

We went to Jaurès' usual café, the Café du Croissant. 'What are the papers saying?' he demanded, and we fell to feverish reading. In *La Sociale* there was an article saying, 'If there was a chief in France who was a man, Jaurès would be put against the wall at the same time as the mobilisation notices.'

'My dear boy,' said Jaurès, who had taken the paper from me when he saw the expression on my face, 'you're forgetting what they taught you at the Lycée and the University, you're not grasping the important point—not that *I* may be put against a wall, but that the mobilisation notices will.'

'When will that be?'

'Tomorrow, in all likelihood. Or the day after. Then—well, I suppose we must expect to be assassinated at any street corner. To love peace is to love Germany in certain twisted minds.'

He began to question people about the hysterical reception given to Poincaré at the Gare du Nord. We went back to the office of *L'Humanité*; he began to write his article for next day's issue—the danger now arose from 'the universal nervousness and sudden impulses, born of fear . . . Therefore, calm, reason! All are invited to the Salle Wagram on Sunday, where resolutions will be passed.'

'It's late,' we said to him, 'and you're tired. Go home tonight by taxi—not by the Metro. You'll need to be on your toes tomorrow.'

So he agreed to go home by taxi. As the cab drove away, its acceleration stirred up a little gust of movement in that normally airless street, brought a sheet of newspaper lying there in the gutter flapping about my ankle. I kicked it away. 'Why, what the devil's *that* doing here?' said someone, laughing. It was a week-old copy of *Action Française*, the ultra-chauvinist newspaper. A line of print caught my eye; 'We have no wish to incite anyone to political assassination but M. Jean Jaurès may well shake in his shoes.'

'What filth they print!' I said, kicking it again, and then again, and then again.

I went home, profoundly depressed. I had telephoned Cousin Amélie to say I should be late, but she was still waiting up for me. 'I knew you would be tired and unhappy,' she said, 'so I've made you a lime-flower *tisane*, it will help you to sleep.'

'How could you be so sure I'd be depressed?'

'Oh,' she said, 'not just because of all this dreadful talk of war, but because of the disgusting way some of these papers talk of Monsieur Jaurès. But you mustn't worry, my dear; after all, this is not Sarajevo, thank God, it's *Paris*!'

But a strange Paris, with hysteria in the air. Even in Paris you could expect the kind of street in which we lived to be silent after midnight, footsteps of a belated homegoer sounding loud and hollow. But throughout that night one could hear, carried on the still air, the noise of distant roar and tumult; the crowds were still out in the main thoroughfares, and even in our quiet street there were constant footsteps, hurried footsteps, and people talking, talking, talking. And, always preponderating, the one word, '*War*.'

The next day dawned brilliantly. I was up soon after five; I must get to Passy to try to persuade him to keep indoors today, tomorrow, the next day. But there he was, coming out of the front door, bent on his morning walk, and all the dejection had fallen away from him. 'I was wrong to doubt—last night I doubted because I was tired. Now, after a good night's sleep, I've got back my mental balance. That I should doubt for a moment the sanity, the good will of workers throughout Europe towards each other!'

'What about the governments, though?'

'Ah, my boy, that's the point, that's the reason I can't stay at home. (I saw the request trembling on your lips from the moment I set eyes on you.) I have to be there, in the thick of things, watching the ministers, above all, Poincaré—they must *know* I'm there, keeping an eye on them, ready to nail the lies I've no doubt are already prepared. Can't you see them working out tactics, Roger? The ordinary worker's nothing more than an animal to them, but they know any animal will fight to the death to defend his mate, his cubs. So invent lies about frontier violations, trumpet that *la patrie*'s in danger, and the animal will react predictably; will wish to protect his own from attack. That's the line to take—flag-wagging won't have any appeal for the poor devils of havenots with nothing to lose, but *attack*— ah, that's different! So I must be there, one voice if no more, to say, "You're lying! The Germans haven't stirred!"'

At the Palais Bourbon, he led a Socialist deputation to the Prime Minister, Viviani. Little satisfaction. But at the newspaper office there was excitement, even hope. There had been a telephone call from Brussels. A German comrade was on his way to Paris. 'That's it!' he said. 'Coolness! Reason! It's not too late! Will the German workers aim their guns at their French brothers?' And then, with little coolness in his voice, but real torment, 'A madman fires two shots in Sarajevo, kills two innocent people, now it seems that the blood of innocent millions is to be spilled. One mad crime is to be followed by something a thousand times more crazed, more criminal! But it can still be averted!'

But the definite news that reached us from Germany seemed shattering. The German government, following Russia's general mobilisation, declared a state of *Kriegsgefahrzustand*. There was wild excitement, panic, above which Jaurès' voice rose, commanding, reassuring.

'Calmness! Reason!' he said. 'What's the use of urging such qualities on our readers if we ourselves lose our wits? In the

71

first place we don't know precisely what this means.' 'Danger of war!' shouted someone. 'The first step to mobilisation!' shouted another.

'Well,' said the star pupil of the Ecole Normale, 'we must find out the exact meaning. I am going to the library of the Chamber of Deputies to look the word up in the best German dictionary available.'

He did so, and decided the best translation was 'State of siege'.

The German messenger arrived. He brought, not hope, but something like despair. Fear of Russia obsessed everyone in Germany. If Socialists were ordered to mobilise against Tsarism, they would obey. But Jaurès did not flinch.

'No, all's not lost! We're still in touch! And there's the meeting called for Sunday—there were anti-war meetings all over France last night, the movement for peace will be like a snowball—no, an avalanche!'

Someone said, 'I could do with an avalanche in this heat.'

People laughed feebly. Even if it had been a good joke and we had been in the mood for it, it was really too hot for laughter. Madame Dubois, the concierge, was sitting on the step, fanning herself against the heat.

'All's not lost!' Jaurès insisted. He had never seemed more vital. 'There'll be riots, barricades! Do you know what I heard in the Chamber today? That when Poincaré was in Russia, he had to go into St Petersburg alone, Tsar Nicholas was afraid to go with him, because of the strikes! Even if Nicholas is an imbecile, he must remember what happened in 1905 after he'd gone to war with Japan, and the strikes hadn't started before the war began then! And Haase told me in Brussels that *his* Kaiser was scared of war. But, above all, we have work to do here, we mustn't bank on everything being done in Berlin and Petersburg!'

It was I who reminded him he had not eaten since the morning. Everyone else with him there at *L'Humanité* office joined in then, saying, yes, he must eat something, but it was I who

72

first said it. 'It's nine o'clock. You haven't eaten since this morning.'

'Very well,' he said. 'The usual place, then.'

'No,' said Jean Longuet, 'not the Café du Croissant. You see too many royalist thugs there. Why not the Coq d'Or?'

'The Coq d'Or, where there's an *orchestra*? How can we talk there? Besides, at the Croissant we're at home. We'll take a taxi, shall we—I know it's just round the corner, but I don't want to be away from the office too long.'

We got into a taxi. It nearly collided with another vehicle. 'Look out, driver!' shouted Longuet, whose nerves were on edge. 'You'll have us all killed!'

The driver gave an astounded look over his shoulder. 'One does not kill Citizen Jaurès,' he said.

Because we arrived late in the Rue Montmartre, there was only one table left at the Croissant, a table before an old sofa set between the windows in a corner nearest the street. It was dreadfully hot—that horrible stale heat you get only in cities. The windows were wide open, but still the café was airless; earlier in the day the sun had been blinding, and they had drawn the little curtain over the windows to keep out the glare. Nobody had bothered to pull the curtain back when the sun disappeared; now it hung down slackly.

Jaurès looked tired. Heat did not trouble him in our own Languedoc, but he always found it trying in cities. We persuaded him therefore to sit on the sofa with his back to the window. He kept checking the time with us; we must not waste a second, back to the office as soon as possible, for the telephone call that might come from Brussels, there might be another emissary from Germany itself. 'He may be there already! Roger, what's the time?'

'Twenty minutes to ten—that's all.'

Somehow he must be induced to eat an adequate meal. In mute conspiracy René Dolié, a journalist from *Bonnet Rouge*, showed him a coloured photograph of his little daughter. Jaurès put out his hand to view it better. 'Let me see it,' he said.

73

From the street another hand pulled back the little curtain. Someone said something like, 'What goes on in here?' There was a flash. Then another.

I thought—and this is the truth, I haven't invented it—'There were two shots at Sarajevo.'

We had leapt to our feet—no, not all of us. *He* hadn't. He'd collapsed sideways on the old sofa by the window. His head fell forward on to the table. We lifted him up, tried to lay him across two unlaid tables, marble-topped tables. He didn't say anything, but he made a gesture, a feeble, helpless gesture with the hand that seconds before had been so strong. Then blood gushed from his head and for a moment I could see his brain beating. 'Napkins,' I said. 'For God's sake, give me all the napkins you can'; I didn't think it would save his life, but I didn't want other people to see what I'd seen. We put the napkins about his head; he did not move, was quite unconscious now. A woman started screaming, 'Jaurès is killed! They have killed Jaurès!'

It was fifteen minutes before he died.

There was a doctor, I recall—no, more than one. They stood shaking their heads—I suppose they must have said something, but I can only remember them standing there shaking their heads.

And there was uproar outside. Someone said the murderer had been caught; the crowd had nearly lynched him.

As they'd nearly lynched the murderer who'd fired the two shots in Sarajevo.

Spilt red wine on the table and red blood, and the walls of the cathedral at Albi were red and after heavy rain the Tarn runs red with detritus. 'Red wine has to breathe before being served'—one of the few things my father had taught me.

The place was suddenly filled with workers from the neighbouring printshops. They thronged the streets outside. Many of them were weeping, but as we carried him out, I saw on all faces one emotion above all—anger.

What should we have done? Stirred them up, like so many Antonys stirring up the people of Rome over dead Caesar's

74

body, so that they rushed away crying, 'Revenge! About! Seek! Burn! Kill! Slay! Let not a traitor live!' so that they burned the Russian Embassy, the Presidential Palace and the Quai d'Orsay to provide his funeral pyre?

Better, perhaps, for France and the world had we done so. But I said—I don't know the exact words—that they should contain their rage, so they stood, heads lowered, teeth clenched, fists clenched, silent, as he passed.

Later we learned that there had been panic in the government when they heard the news. The Prefect of Police telephoned to say there would be revolution in Paris within three hours, the slums would rise, he had asked that the cavalry ordered forward that night should stay instead in Paris.

A minister had exclaimed, 'A foreign war and a civil war!'

They closed the Rue de Grenelle to the public to keep the crowds from reaching the Russian Embassy; rumours were spreading that the murder was the work of the Russian Secret Police. But Jaurès was in fact struck down by the unbalanced son of a mad mother, who had just come to Paris after attending the funeral of a mad grandmother. He was a great reader of nationalist newspapers.

Poor Madame Dubois, the concierge, was to come to me, weeping. She had been sitting on the doorstep of the office when a fair-haired stranger came up. 'Is Monsieur Jaurès here?' 'I told him nobody was here, told him where you'd all gone. *I told him where to find Monsieur Jaurès, monsieur!*' Poor soul, taking on her thin shoulders the guilt that was others'.

There were immense crowds as Jaurès' body was carried through the streets. Two details I remember quite clearly. The cries of *'Chapeaux bas!'* that were raised as we approached. And then, as we actually passed, a tremendous clamour, 'Jaurès! Jaurès.' And—this I'll never forget—*'Vive Jaurès!* Jaurès, live! Jaurès, you cannot be dead! *Jaurès, we deny that you are dead— if we will not admit it, if we deny it strongly enough, it will not have happened! Don't weep yet, shout "Jaurès! Vive Jaurès!" and please God, if we shout loudly enough, we'll wake the dead!'*

75

'*Jaurès! Vive Jaurès!*'

But he does not awaken.

The next day a second German messenger arrived. A Belgian came, too, I remember. With four of Jaurès' colleagues they sat in the Palais Bourbon, the Chamber of Deputies, its corridors now boiling with furious hatred against Germany.

They sat, and they talked. They talked with little hope. Hope had died with Jaurès. There was little more life in them than there was in him now.

I met them as they came away. They moved like sleepwalkers. What were they going to do? At least the Socialists in both French and German parliaments could refuse to vote war credits! Couldn't they issue a joint manifesto to this effect?

They looked at me, dull-eyed. 'That can't be done. There's no longer any telegraphic communication between Paris and Berlin.'

So, on technical grounds, the joint operation was abandoned. And forty million men would fight sixty million.

'We must get to the station,' said the German and the Belgian.

But how to get to the station? On that Saturday afternoon, still blisteringly hot, Paris was deathly quiet.

'Taxis?'

'There are no taxis.'

'We'll go to the Metro.'

'It's not running.'

'A bus, then.'

'They're requisitioned to carry meat to the Army.'

They hurried away to find whatever means of transport was available. I stood irresolute outside the Palais Bourbon. A clock struck; four o'clock. There was a slapping noise behind me. It sounded quite loud in the stillness. An old man with a brush and a bundle of posters under his arm.

And there it went up on the wall of the Palais Bourbon, the shining poster.

> *'Armée de Terre et Armée de Mer*
> *Ordre de Mobilisation Générale.'*

I still could not believe it, although I touched the poster when it was still damp.

'A shame about Citizen Jaurès,' the old bill-poster said to me.

I too became part of the Army. Not, as my father might have forgiven me for, as a *cuirassier* splendid in blue and steel, but as a stretcher-bearer. Miraculously I have survived so far, but the luck can't go on much longer. When you are helping to carry a stretcher you can't throw yourself to the ground when you hear a shell coming. So I must get this all down while there is still time.

And, possibly, while there still exists the faintest flicker of hope that one day there will be an end to the fratricide, and survivors will be able to 'walk and sing and meditate under the sky', and there may be grass and flowers over the 'fields of martyrs' that make up the battleground of Verdun.

4

Upon St Olga's Day

Russia 1914

Two men, Generals Dobrorolsky and Tatischev, never forgot
any detail in the sequence of events following that day.* For the
first that sequence represented definite professional achievement
—after some hours of agonising frustration. The account he was
to write seven years later, without access to notes or papers,
showed only a few slips of memory, those only of a minor variety.

The second man did not have so long a period for remem-
brance, and never set down his recollections. In any case, it is
doubtful whether he would have wished to do so.

During the War of Liberation against Napoleon, the close
relationship between the Tsar and the King of Prussia had been
given a formal expression that was to endure until this summer
of 1914. The two monarchs had exchanged personal adjutants;
in 1914 the German *Flügeladjutanten* in St Petersburg was
General Chelius; the Tsar's personal representative at the
German court, General Tatischev, happened to be on leave in
Russia during this critical time.

He was a grey-bearded, tall, spare, eagle-nosed cavalry officer
of the old school. He had made an excellent impression in
Berlin, both on the courtiers and the excitable Kaiser, who
favoured him with confidences the well-bred Tatischev often
found embarrassing, but which he endured partly because he
had come to realise, with some concern, that Wilhelm was
becoming scared of his own General Staff—and therefore, like
a scared small boy, bragged and boasted.

* July 11, 1914 in Russia, July 24 in Western Europe.

'He has never grown up,' a very old general had once confided in a low voice to Tatischev. 'Never got beyond the Potsdam lieutenant. You know what Bismarck said of him—he wants to celebrate his birthday every day.'

'Ah, Bismarck!' sighed an elderly diplomat who, fortunately perhaps, had caught only the name of the Iron Chancellor. '*He* could keep you damned soldiers in your proper place! Nobody else has managed to do it.'

Tatischev was to reflect on this in the hot July of 1914, reflect painfully that it did not apply merely to Germany.

When he had come to Russia on leave, he had reported at once to the Tsar. There had been two points he had tried to stress particularly, the feeling of tension in Berlin, nerves on the stretch, the air charged with electricity, only a spark needed to provoke an explosion, and a new note in the Kaiser's voice, a note almost of fear, a new look, almost haggard, on the nervous face.

The Tsar had listened with apparently intent, unwavering attention—that, as Tatischev knew, often concealed sheer apathy.

'You mean they are preparing for war?' he asked. 'I was told the same thing by Kokovtsov* last November.' After a moment he added, 'Well, God's will be done.'

'No, sir,' Tatischev had said, 'I mean that *they* are convinced that there is tremendous pressure here and in France to begin a war against *them*.'

The Tsar had not been listening. 'I can speak to you with frankness. We both know the Kaiser is—what's the word?—an exhibitionist, but he doesn't want war.'

'I know, sir, but he's afraid of appearing weak,' said Tatischev. 'He knows the current gossip that he lost his nerve on the occasions in the past when a fair-minded observer might say he acted as a friend of peace. I myself on manoeuvres in Silesia two years ago heard German officers saying, "We'll see to it that it doesn't happen again." His Majesty is only human, after all;

* The former Prime Minister, dismissed in January 1914.

79

many rash actions are taken solely because people are afraid of being called cowards.'

Again he hesitated, wondering whether he had gone too far, whether the Emperor sitting before him might take this analysis of the character of the Emperor in Berlin as an indirect criticism of his own temperament. But the Tsar merely sighed and remarked that all was in God's hands. Tatischev wondered if he had sat through the whole audience sunk in boredom, or whether behind the appearance of close attention there had been, not simple *ennui*, but literal absence of mind, thoughts elsewhere, in the upper storey of the palace where the young Heir to the throne, it was rumoured, was ill again. Certainly he had seen and heard nothing of the Empress, who usually received him when he returned to Russia. She would, Tatischev imagined gloomily, be doubly distraught now—her adored son was ill, and Rasputin, the malodorous peasant she believed had been sent by God to save her son, was not in Petersburg.

Tatischev lunched with the Imperial suite, and was briefed by them. The Tsar's family had embarked on their summer cruise in the Imperial yacht *Standart*, but the *Standart*, having too great a draught for an embarkation at Peterhof, had waited at Kronstadt, and the Family had been taken out to her in the small steam-yacht, *Alexandria*. As they were going aboard, the Heir had jumped at the wrong moment, so that his ankle caught the bottom of the ladder leading to the deck. At the time people thought that no damage had been done, but by evening the internal bleeding had begun, and the boy had had a bad night.

Tatischev's informant said, 'None of them appeared for luncheon; I was picking at this and that when I realised that there was a state of excitement at the end of the table which was spreading in my direction. "What's wrong?" I asked. "Nothing's wrong," muttered old Nilov, "wonderful news, in fact. My dear fellow, you know that that scoundrel—" (I spare you the term he usually applies to Rasputin) "went back to his dirty Siberian village for a visit? Well, he's had a knife stuck in him—by a woman, of course."

' "Is he badly hurt?"

' "Well, a knife-wound in the guts isn't something to shrug off." Nilov stared round the table. "Nine-tenths of us hope he's done for, but daren't show it, of course. The others—damned fools of women—say he's bound to recover because he's sent from God." '

'My own feeling,' concluded Tatischev's informant, 'is that he'll live—not, believe me, from wishful thinking—but from the gloomy conviction that the devil looks after his own.'

Tatischev contemplated the situation as he travelled back to St Petersburg. The Tsar, returning from his cruise, was being confronted with possibly the greatest of crises following the assassination of the heir to the Austrian throne. Normally, he would never have dreamed of doing anything without consulting his wife, and *she* would do nothing without asking the advice of Rasputin. But now Rasputin, who would have opposed any idea of war, would be out of action for weeks, and the Tsarina would be absorbed in her son's illness.

The Tsar would have to stand alone.

'On July 11, St Olga's Day,' General Sergei Dobrorolsky wrote seven years later in exile in Belgrade, 'between eleven o'clock and noon, the Chief of the General Staff, General Janushkevitch, called me on the service telephone and told me to come immediately to his office.'

The general walked briskly to his superior's room. Janushkevitch, forty-four years old, with black moustache, black curly hair, but, unusually for a Russian general of the period, no beard, was almost shaking with excitement.

'The situation is very serious,' he started saying before Dobrorolsky had even closed the door. 'Austria has delivered a wholly unacceptable ultimatum to the Serbian Government.'

Dobrorolsky made the odd clicking noise, half irritation, half dismay, that always intrigued visitors to Russia. It could be very useful; it indicated a reaction, but did not commit as far as an articulate response might do.

'We intend to make our position clear,' continued Janush-kevitch, his dramatic tones rather wasted on an audience of one. 'We'll have a short official warning published tomorrow. We shall state that all Russia is watching with the closest attention the course of the negotiations between Austria and Serbia and we will not remain inactive if the dignity and integrity of our blood brothers, the Serbian people, are threatened!'

'Quite,' said Dobrorolsky. He had heard it all before, read it all before. There was really no new comment one could make. But then the Chief of Staff seated himself at his desk and assumed the look of Man of Destiny.

'Have you everything ready for the mobilisation proclamation?' demanded Janushkevitch.

Dobrorolsky felt excitement clutching at the pit of his stomach. As stage manager he had planned so hard, rehearsed so often—was this to be the real performance, this time they marched? He nodded. Janushkevitch, relishing his own rôle, threw himself back in his chair, and, addressing the ceiling rather than the Chief of the Mobilisation Section, ordered, 'In an hour bring me all the documents relative to the preparing of our troops for war!' And then spoiled the effect by adding hastily, and with some nervousness, 'Partial mobilisation against Austria only, of course! We mustn't give Germany any cause for believing *she's* being threatened.'

'But partial mobilisation is absolutely out of the question,' said Dobrorolsky.

'The decision has been made,' said Janushkevitch, back in Ercles' vein. (This was to prove a day of Shakespearian themes.) 'A detailed report in an hour, please.'

Dobrorolsky left him opening a box of chocolates. The Chief of Staff did not smoke or offer cigarettes to callers. They and he were sustained on chocolates. Most visitors found this rather disconcerting. 'He shouldn't really do it,' thought Dobrorolsky. 'It gives a bad impression. He ought to know that a lot of people think he shouldn't have the job, being so young.'

The Minister of War himself had said the Chief of Staff was

'still a child'—yet he had secured Janushkevitch's appointment only a few months ago, the sixth appointment to the post since the General Staff had lost its independence to the War Ministry six years before. 'If only we had some consistency of planning!' the hard-pressed Dobrorolsky had groaned in his heart often enough—and particularly on the eve of the departure of a new Chief of Staff for a conference with French allies who always made exorbitant demands or fantastic assumptions as to what Russia was capable of—and no Russian Chief of Staff, shaking about uneasily in his new boots, ever liked to appear disobliging to his hosts—or to make any statement that would appear to contradict the bland optimism of the War Minister, who alone enjoyed access to the Tsar. The despondent toilers of the seven hundred and sixty-eight windowed office of the General Staff never knew to what fresh lunacies they would be committed by a Chief of Staff's return from France.

If only Danilov were here! But Danilov, Janushkevitch's stern, taciturn deputy, was away on a tour of the Caucasus. Danilov knew this idiotic idea of partial mobilisation was impossible to accept, Janushkevitch would listen to Danilov if to no one else. Would there be any point in getting hold of Rozhnin, Chief of Military Transportation? Rozhnin knew the idea of a partial mobilisation was lunacy, could not be done, but only Danilov could make Janushkevitch change his mind. Still, just as well to see Rozhnin, to talk over things.

'The politicians have got at him,' was Rozhnin's first reaction to Dobrorolsky's news. 'The best thing that could ever happen to *us* would be removal from this damned building.'

For the three-storeyed building that was officially the Office of the General Staff also housed the Ministries of Finance and Foreign Affairs.

'Long-nosed Sazonov working overtime?' asked Dobrorolsky. 'Wasn't he up until God knows when this morning saying goodbye to the French?'

The French President Poincaré had just left Petersburg after a State visit.

Rozhnin suddenly whistled. 'Clever timing! The Austrians waited until Poincaré'd left before presenting their ultimatum! Anyhow, let's see what we can find out—I've a young fellow here who has a close friend in the Foreign Ministry—shared the same English governess! I'll send him scouting. He shouldn't be long—have you time to wait?'

Dobrorolsky shrugged. 'He told me to be back in an hour. It's a waste of an hour. You know as well as I do—partial mobilisation's technically impossible!'

Rozhnin's young fellow did his job quickly. Sazonov, the Foreign Minister, who had only got to bed long after midnight, had been roused at seven o'clock with a telegram from Belgrade giving details of the Austrian ultimatum. When he arrived at his Ministry at ten, Sazonov, presumably still influenced by the recent State visit, had greeted one of his colleagues with, *'C'est la guerre Européenne!'* The Foreign Minister had telephoned the Tsar; later he told people that His Imperial Majesty's reaction had been, 'This is disturbing.'

The Foreign Minister had arranged a meeting of the Council of Ministers that afternoon at three, and had seen Janushkevitch on the spot.

'Partial mobilisation is technically impossible!' declared Dobrorolsky, repeating his affirmation of faith.

'Well,' said Rozhnin slowly, 'if *partial* mobilisation's technically impossible—'

Their eyes met. Rozhnin, suddenly remembering that the 'young fellow' was still there, waved him away, but the boy possessed intelligence enough to interpret the sudden glance. He was, it also appeared, a brash youth, for as he saluted and made for the door, he showed that some at least of his English governess's teaching had borne fruit, by declaiming,

> 'This day is call'd the feast of Olga.
> He that outlives this day, and comes safe home,
> Will stand a tip-toe when this day is named,
> And rouse him at the name of Olga.'

'Get along with you, you young scoundrel!' said Rozhnin, laughing. 'And lower your voice.'

He lowered his voice so that all that Dobrorolsky caught as the door closed, was:

'—That fought with us upon St Olga's day!' but once outside brashness took over again. There was actually a burst of song, words chanted to the tune of the *Marseillaise*:

> '*Cette fois nous marcherons,*
> *Formant nos bataillons.*'

Rozhnin burst out laughing. 'What a marvellous time to be young! I can't call him back and reprimand him! My heart wouldn't be in it.'

For, of course, it was all or nothing. A civilian, Sazonov, was trying to make use of partial mobilisation as a diplomatic bluff, to scare Austria. And it wouldn't work. This—and the reasons for it—Dobrorolsky set down in painstaking detail when he returned to his office. War between Austria and Russia would inevitably involve Germany, and so no mobilisation plan had ever been worked out that involved Austria alone.

But it was never possible, thought Dobrorolsky pessimistically, to explain to any civilian the difficulties of the mechanics of war. All one could do was to stress that certain things were technically impossible, which the politicians should accept, even if they could not understand. Strategy was too serious a thing to be comprehended by the civilians.

It did not occur to him that a civilian might one day retort that such inability to overcome a technical difficulty was surely a sign of incompetence.

It was stiflingly hot in St Petersburg. All who could, left the city for their summer holidays. By the following day, a Saturday, the capital was almost deserted. But Dobrorolsky grimly stuck to his post, never far away from the telephone, as night fell switching on his green-shaded lamp to stare at maps he already knew by heart, to calculate numbers he already knew by heart, to repeat again and again, as a priest rehearsing the Articles of Belief, 'Partial mobilisation is technically impossible. It's general mobilisation or nothing.'

General mobilisation would mean war.

Russia could not back down. She had backed down some years before, when Austria had annexed Bosnia. She could not back down again.

Dobrorolsky was a kindly man. He was genuinely disturbed when, on his way back to the office after lunch on St Olga's Day, he saw an unfortunate cart-horse, dragging sacks of flour through the heat, drop dead. Thereafter when he passed the Troitsky Bridge he eyed with deep concern the weary horses trying to drag carts up the steep incline. Most of the poor beasts looked half-starved.

Scandalous to send poor starving dumb brutes toiling through such heat, thought Dobrorolsky in disgust, then returned to his airless office and cogitation as to how infantry might be sent marching to the enemy frontier in double-quick time.

Dobrorolsky spent the days following St Olga's Day expostulating in airless offices, against a rustling background of maps being rolled and unrolled, the riffling through of the pages of code books, that partial mobilisation was technically impossible. Tatischev, attending the Tsar, had a broader stage for his more muted asseveration that mobilisation, because it must lead to war, was unthinkable.

One scene was set against the great plain of Krassnoe Selo, baked iron hard by the burning sun, the smoke from distant forest fires like a cloud on the horizon. Here the Tsar held the Ministerial Council that decided on mobilisation against Austria.

It had been a mistake to hold the Council at Krassnoe, thought Tatischev, shifting uneasily in his chair. The place was alive with soldiers gathered for the summer review by the Tsar. 'It's good to be here, surrounded by my soldiers,' the Tsar had said to him that morning. But looking at the slight figure in the President's chair, seemingly weighted down by its epauletted tunic and decorations, one did not think 'the Tsar surrounded by his soldiers'; instead one thought, 'the Tsar *isolated* among his soldiers'.

And another Emperor, like his cousin in Berlin, terribly afraid that his soldiers would think him afraid.

The argument was three-cornered. Sazonov argued in favour of partial mobilisation as a diplomatic bluff against Austria. The soldiers argued for general mobilisation. Anything less would be disastrous. One should be logical, far-sighted. War between Serbia and Austria meant war between Russia and Austria. War between Russia and Austria meant war between Russia and Germany. War—which meant for Russia a heaven-sent opportunity to have her final reckoning with Germany and Austria and to acquire Constantinople—was inevitable. Therefore the sooner general mobilisation was ordered, the better.

Another argument was also advanced. St Petersburg was in the grip of a strike by the workers. Mobilisation was the best way of dealing with this internal danger, just as it was the best way of dealing with the external situation. Mobilisation, in fact, was the universal panacea for all evils.

The Tsar asked hesitantly whether industrial unrest, such as undoubtedly existed, might not lead to 'complications' in case of mobilisation—and the probable result of mobilisation.

No, he was answered. Industrial unrest did not present any problem or obstacle whatsoever. War would rally the whole country behind the throne. War was the best way of defeating the enemy within. This was the line taken by Maklakov, the Minister of the Interior. Just over ten years before, Maklakov's predecessor had prescribed a 'small, victorious war' as the remedy for the country's ills; the result had been catastrophic defeat at the hands of Japan, an assassin's bomb for the minister, near-revolution throughout the country. No one but Tatischev seemed to remember this. And Tatischev, present at the Council by decree of the Tsar, was not empowered to speak. The only man who opposed the idea of war was the aged Count Fredericks, Minister of the Court. The old man had been failing for years, but had been retained in office because the Tsar did not want to hurt him by dismissing him. The Count's rambling pleas for caution, his shaking voice, provoked shrugs of irritation, not too covert sneers. His advocacy of peace was punctuated by shouts of command from the review ground. Eventually he became aware of the unconcealed impatience about him, and sat down slowly. To Tatischev, seated behind him, he turned puzzled eyes and said unhappily, 'It seems that from today if you speak in favour of peace you're branded as pro-German.'

Tatischev nodded, and looked round at the flushed, angry faces. A loud voice again passionately began to declaim the idiot equation, 'War between Austria and Serbia means war between Austria and Russia, and war between Russia and Austria means war between Russia and Germany,' and there was applause.

'War with Germany,' thought Tatischev, 'really means war with the Prussian General Staff. Meticulously detailed planning. Infinite research. Backed by superbly efficient railways and Krupps. And we have a War Minister who believes in the supremacy of lance and bayonet.'

After the meeting, the review and manoeuvres were cut short; it was announced that similarly manoeuvres throughout the Russian Empire were to be curtailed and troops were to return to standing quarters—as they would in case of war.

There would really be no need to stick up the red mobilisation notices to tell the world what was being planned.

Cadets of the St Petersburg Military Academy were immediately promoted to the rank of regular officers in the Army, instead of waiting until the end of the year. The fodder being fed to the cannon that summer would be green, the sap still in it.

A banquet followed at Krassnoe. The Russian officers seemed in the grip of a collective dementia. It was perhaps not surprising that the newly promoted cadets should swagger and bluster, especially after gulping down too much champagne.

'Now,' they kept calling out to each other across the table, 'we're *starting* something!'

But their seniors were just as bad. Tatischev heard the military governor of St Petersburg actually mentioning mobilisation when talking to General Chelius, the German officer attached to the Tsar's suite in the same capacity as he himself was attached to the Kaiser.

When the banquet ended, Chelius, a pleasant, cultivated man, sought out Tatischev. 'I did not know madness was a contagious disease,' he said.

'When does your Emperor's cruise end?' asked Tatischev—the Kaiser was at sea in his yacht.

'What's today? Saturday—one loses count of time these days. He should be back on Monday. Please God after that all *this* will seem nothing more than a bad dream.'

When, shortly afterwards, the army at Krassnoe broke camp and marched off into the twilight, it seemed an army of so many grey ghosts, tramping and riding from the shadows of one nightmare into the shadows of another. All that night the beat of hooves echoed and re-echoed through Tatischev's brain.

But this, after all, remained only partial mobilisation.

General Danilov returned on the following day. He was in no doubt as to what would happen. He had telegraphed his wife and family to come to Petersburg—they had been staying near the Austrian frontier. Dobrorolsky felt quite light-headed with relief at Danilov's return; and the prospect of unswerving support from that most formidable of men; this damned partial mobilisation, meant to scare off Austria, couldn't scare off a paralytic grandmother, as it was *technically impossible*. But at least at ten past four on the afternoon of the 25th Dobrorolsky had been empowered to send out a secret telegram presaging better things. 'Prepare quickly transport plans and provisions for the return of all troops to standing quarters—' Not exactly general mobilisation, but a first step in that direction.

Yet there remained disturbing hints of weakness—dare one even, as a loyal subject, say *obtuseness*—in quarters higher than the Foreign Ministry. A German merchant ship at Kronstadt was thought to be acting suspiciously, its wireless was seized, and the vessel was forbidden to leave harbour. The German Ambassador protested, and the Tsar himself had intervened, ordering the freeing of the ship, condemning the whole incident.

It was difficult not to be depressed by such an episode. The General found himself positively brooding upon it as he walked away from the General Staff building (his wife had persuaded him he must stretch his legs from time to time; he'd ruin his health cooped up all those hours in such heat). He decided to take a turn in the Summer Gardens, but afterwards wished he had not. All the children left in St Petersburg seemed to have been taken there to play on the wide, shady paths, but even the trees brought little relief from the torrid heat, no leaf stirred, the children were whining and fretful, the air seemed filled with their crying.

There was a small white terrier tethered outside the Gardens (to which dogs, like private soldiers, were not admitted). It was whimpering when the General went in, and when he came out again, had collapsed with heat exhaustion. In genuine indignation he ordered a startled passer-by to go into the Gardens and find the animal's owner. It was bad enough when illiterate owners of cart-horses showed unthinking cruelty, he fumed, but far worse when presumably educated people showed such crassness.

Even strolling beside the river brought no refreshment; the Neva lay in the torrid sun looking like oily copper. No breeze came upstream, only the acrid smell of forest fires burning in Finland.

General Dobrorolsky, on his way back to make plans for the partial mobilisation he hoped in his heart would never be carried out, took what relief he could before turning into his office from taking a good look at the bronze group of Victory in a six-horse chariot that surmounted the building.

He was to write seven years later in Belgrade that from the moment Sazonov was informed of the Austrian ultimatum, *'Voina byla uzhe predrieshena'*—the war was already a settled matter. But others did not see it so. It was only four days later, when Austria, having rejected the Serbian answer to her ultimatum, declared war, that Sazonov, as Dobrorolsky put it, saw sense, realised that not only war, but general war, was inevitable, sent for Janushkevitch, and said general mobilisation must be proceeded with immediately, expressed astonishment, indeed, that it had not begun sooner.

That evening Janushkevitch held a meeting with Danilov, Dobrorolsky, Rozhnin. He too was quite won over to the idea that only general mobilisation was possible, and would go out to Peterhof to see the Tsar next morning. But it would be best to take with him two mobilisation ukases, one, for general mobilisation, was to receive the Imperial signature if it were at all possible; the notice for partial mobilisation would be used only if His Majesty still maintained the attitude he had shown in the case of the German merchant vessel.

The windows were open. Huge moths fluttered in and blundered about the lamps. One fell, a singed lump, on to the table before Dobrorolsky. It was not a very pleasant sight; he tried to think of it as a withered leaf. Before the leaves so still on the boughs in the Summer Gardens fell, where would the soldiers forbidden to enter those gardens be? In Berlin? He felt suddenly so excited at the thought he had to excuse himself. Disconcerting that excitement—pleasurable excitement—could produce the same physical effects as craven fear.

And Janushkevitch, going out to Peterhof the following morning, came, saw, conquered so completely that he came back with the Tsar's signature to both ukases—'He said he'd sign the second one in case there was some improvement in the diplomatic situation,' he said, laughing, to Dobrorolsky.

'Voina byla uzhe predrieshena,' repeated Dobrorolsky solemnly. Janushkevitch in buoyant reaction, however, was in the mood

for a little light comedy. He sent for the German Military Attaché, Major Eggeling. For a time, however, it seemed that Eggeling would not play his part. The most punctual of men did not present himself at the stipulated moment. But eventually he turned up, an hour late, and, observed the scandalised Dobrorolsky, wearing not uniform, but civilian clothes. Janushkevitch's own satisfaction was muted by another departure from Eggeling's usual behaviour; previously the Attaché always had spoken Russian: now he kept obstinately to French; it meant that Janushkevitch, whose command of French fell short of absolute mastery, was denied some of the finer nuances of irony in their conversation. Eggeling, in French, expressed blunt suspicion. He had heard that reserves in the Warsaw and Vilna districts were being called up. 'On the word of an officer, such reports are absolutely without foundation,' said Janushkevitch. 'A false alarm here, another there—you know how it all builds up.'

Eggeling remained stubbornly unconvinced.

'Of course I can give no guarantee for the future—but who can?' continued Janushkevitch. 'I can, however, give you my most solemn word of honour—and if you like I'll put it in writing—that up to this moment no mobilisation has taken place anywhere, not a man, not a horse. I can also assure you that His Imperial Majesty doesn't want mobilisation.'

'I hope it remains so,' said Eggeling heavily. 'Your mobilisation means war automatically. If a man has a pistol in his pocket, he won't let it remain there while an enemy pistol is being placed at his forehead.'

Janushkevitch did not offer him a chocolate.

'Well, it was true enough,' Janushkevitch said to Dobrorolsky when the interview was over, 'His Majesty doesn't want mobilisation, although he's agreed to it! And mobilisation hasn't been announced yet, the ukase was sitting innocuously in my pocket as I spoke. But not a moment longer. Here it is—now, my friend, it's up to you to get the necessary signatures as soon as possible!'

Dobrorolsky was inexpressibly moved as he took the document with the Imperial signature. This was to be present at the making of history! It was rather a pity that Janushkevitch, with no appreciation of the heroic moment, was scrabbling in a freshly opened box for chocolates to sustain him after his exertions.

And now Dobrorolsky was not merely present at the making of history; he himself must play an active part. The mobilisation order must be countersigned by the Ministers of War, the Navy and the Interior, so first along to Isaac Square and the triangular War Office, and the short, obese, petulant War Minister and a surprise—not, thank God, the worst of surprises, refusal to sign, but reluctance—definite reluctance. 'It really shattered me,' Dobrorolsky said afterwards—that Sukhomlinov, who in the past had been ready to order general mobilisation on what one might almost call the most frivolous pretext (once on the eve of going off with his young, expensive wife for a holiday on the French Riviera) should now—well, show signs of heavy-heartedness at the prospect of war, strained credulity. Tiredness, such as Sukhomlinov also exhibited, was not surprising; having a wife thirty-two years his junior left him puffy-eyed and yawning most of his days. But depression—and, amazingly, when Dobrorolsky, trying to cheer him, referred to a recently published article of the most bellicose nature the Minister had written, entitled *Russia is Ready*, Sukhomlinov grunted out something that might even be interpreted as regret—well, that really was something. 'Gentlemen,' Dobrorolsky was to tell colleagues in the days that followed, 'I was shattered, completely shattered!'

But at least the War Minister signed. The gold bracelets he affected jangled as he did so like a miniature tocsin. 'Well,' said Sukhomlinov, attempting to square meaty shoulders tightly encased in uniform, 'of man-power we have enough, thank God!'

'The nation in arms,' he added vaguely. 'The nation at war. Would you like a drink, my dear fellow?'

Dobrorolsky excused himself. He wondered whether he dared explain to the Minister that there was a difference between the two phrases—a nation at war surely meant that one section *behind* the lines supplied with food and weapons the actual fighting men. But Sukhomlinov was rambling on. 'The Napoleonic concept!' he exclaimed, in an attempt to cheer himself.

Only the previous year the Minister had dismissed five instructors at the Staff College who had viciously persisted in lecturing about fire-tactics. Surely the Corsican had always paid minute attention to fire power? And it had been the French Revolutionaries who'd hit upon the idea of the nation in arms—

Pondering on such historic topics, Dobrorolsky hurried on the next stage of his historic mission. But at the yellow and white Admiralty, with its gilded spire, he met with disappointment—Admiral Grigorovitch was away, would not be back until seven o'clock; Dobrorolsky's only reaction for the moment was to muse with some exasperation, but also a modicum of whimsicality, that it was to be hoped that his quest would not prove so arduous as that of the girl in that novel by Scott that had been such a favourite of his mother's. What had she done? Walked all the way from Scotland to London for some reason or other—getting a reprieve from a death sentence, that was it.

Hardly, however, a historic mission like obtaining the signatures for general mobilisation.

Dobrorolsky made his way to the Tchernuishovskaya Square and the Ministry of the Interior. He was taken immediately to the Minister, Maklakov, who, it was alleged, partly maintained himself in office by his gift for animal mimicry which entranced the Imperial children, the Minister's forte being his imitation of a love-sick panther.

Here, assuredly, there would be no hesitation; Dobrorolsky had heard all about the line taken by Maklakov at the Ministerial Council. Yet he found the Minister still brooding upon internal dangers—but gloomily.

'With us,' said Maklakov, 'the war can't be popular deep down among the masses of the people. Revolutionary ideas mean more to them than talk of victory over Germany—'

There was little of the side-splitting imitator of panthers about him now. He sat at a table upon which he had set ikons, ritual lamps. Beside these Dobrorolsky mutely placed the Imperial ukase. Maklakov looked at him, sighed, crossed himself and said heavily, 'We cannot escape our fate.'

And so he added his signature.

Now all that was needful was the signature of the errant Admiral. A few more hours of waiting, and Dobrorolsky had it.

And so to the General Telegraph Office—number 15 in the Potchtamtskaya. The Chief Director of the Post and Telegraph had been notified in advance that a message of extraordinary importance was to be transmitted; Dobrorolsky entered the private office, handed over the telegram form and said, 'I'll wait to see it sent off.'

He must be present personally at the transmission of the mobilisation order to the four corners of the Russian Empire. It was half past nine in the evening.

First several girls sat down at typewriters to click off copies of the telegram so that transmission should be simultaneous to all military centres. The rest of the office was absolutely silent; during the transmission of the mobilisation telegrams no other messages of any sort could be sent.

They went into the great transmission room. There, at their keys, sat a dozen operators, waiting for the completed forms.

It was, thought Dobrorolsky, preparing to hand over the typed copies, like an orchestra waiting for the conductor to bring down his baton at the commencement of an overture.

Or like a line of guns awaiting the order to fire?

He took a deep breath. *This* was the making of history.

A post office employee ran into the room, up to the Director.

'Are you mad?' the latter demanded. 'Strictest orders were given that under no circumstances whatsoever were we to be interrupted—'

'Sir! An urgent message has just come through—the Chief of Staff himself on the telephone—must speak to General Dobrorolsky—'

'Wait!' said Dobrorolsky in a voice he himself would never have recognised.

Back to the Director's private office, the ominous black receiver lying on the desk.

'Has the message been sent?'

'I was just giving the copies to the operators.'

'Hold them back until Tugan-Baranovsky arrives. He'll tell you everything—I can't over the telephone.'

Suspended animation, deliberate suspension of thought for Dobrorolsky until the Staff-Captain, Tugan-Baranovsky, arrived, panting. 'I've hurried after you through the city, sir. A special order from the Tsar.'

The order was for the suspension of general mobilisation. Instead, partial mobilisation was to be adopted.

'But they must all know it's technically impossible,' said Dobrorolsky, but without heat, and quite automatically.

Equally automatically, he went back into the imposing transmission room, took back the order for general mobilisation and all the typed copies, officially notified the head of the telegraph office that the withdrawal had taken place. After this, he was to write seven years later, he rode away. One is left with the impression that he returned immediately to the office of the General Staff, but first he stopped outside the Admiralty and sat staring at it silently.

If only Grigorovitch hadn't gone off on his damned jaunt, the message would have been sent hours before—

'Sir, are you all right?' came the alarmed voice of Tugan-Baranovsky, who had accompanied him.

Dobrorolsky found to his horror that like a child he was knuckling tear-filled eyes.

'It's the smoke from those damned forest fires,' he said. 'It stings.'

Tugan-Baranovsky, too diplomatically, murmured something about everyone being in need of a good night's sleep too.

'I've just remembered something,' said Dobrorolsky. 'Get on back—say I'll be there in five minutes.'

All he did with his five minutes was to go down to the river, still rubbing his eyes. There were few about to see him; the intense heat still kept most people out of the city, and the opal dimness of a Petersburg summer night did not make for clarity. If you looked up or down stream the bridges themselves were as blurred as shadows. About him moved only a few couples, lovers clasping hands. A few feet from the general stood a young man quoting Pushkin to a girl, 'No, I don't want to die, I want to live, to think, to suffer—'

Dobrorolsky did not hear him. He went on rubbing his eyes, thinking, 'If only Grigorovitch hadn't gone off on his damned jaunt—'

He was to receive many congratulations seven years later because he remembered the events of that day with such amazing accuracy. But recollection had been etched on his memory by acid.

The Kaiser, on his return, had acted. He telegraphed to his cousin the Russian Tsar that all sovereigns should insist on the punishment of the Serbian assassins of the Archduke Franz Ferdinand. 'In this case politics play no part at all. I am exerting my utmost influence to induce the Austrians . . . to arrive at a satisfactory understanding with you. I confidently hope you will help me in my efforts to smooth over difficulties that may still arise.'

The Tsar sent for Tatischev, who found the usually dreamy blue eyes were glowing with excitement. The Emperor had an idea—why not submit the whole Austro-Serbian dispute to the Hague Tribunal, his own creation? An excellent idea, said Tatischev, but, time being all-important, would it not be as well in the meantime to try to build—as it were—a bridge for peace with the Kaiser's assistance? The Tsar agreed, and sent a telegram which, had he possessed imagination enough to see it, betrayed dreadfully his own weakness.

'Am glad you are back. In this most serious moment, I appeal to you to help me . . . The indignation in Russia shared fully by me is enormous. I foresee that very soon I shall be over-whelmed by the pressure brought upon me and be forced to take extreme measures which will lead to war—'

And on the stiflingly hot evening when Dobrorolsky, having waited for so long for the signature of Admiral Grigorovitch, at last began to make his way to the General Telegraph Office, the Tsar received the Kaiser's reply.

'. . . Of course military measures on the part of Russia which would be looked on by Austria as threatening would precipitate a calamity we both wish to avoid and jeopardise my position as mediator . . .'

So the Kaiser telegraphed at 6.40 in the evening. The Tsar received the telegram at 9.30. Hours before he had signed the mobilisation ukase; he turned desperately to Tatischev—was it too late? There was only one way of finding out, Tatischev must telephone the War Minister immediately, said the Tsar. After a moment's silence Tatischev said, 'With respect, sir, the order to cancel the general mobilisation must come from Your Imperial Majesty yourself—we haven't a moment to lose.'

So the Tsar, accompanied by Tatischev and Fredericks, went down to the hall of the palace where the telephone stood, and in person gave the order to countermand the general mobilisation. He needed instructions of both a technical and a tactical kind from his servants. 'You must help me—I'm unused to the instrument,' and then, as they were making the connection for him, 'How shall I put what I have to say?'

The two tall men exchanged glances over his head. 'Sir,' said Tatischev, 'time's all-important. You must say immediately that the general mobilisation is to be cancelled.'

But, characteristically, the Tsar chose another method of

approach. Once he heard Sukhomlinov's amazed voice at the other end, he first read the text of the Kaiser's telegram to the War Minister, and only after this said—asking a question, and not giving an order: 'Is it then really impossible to hold up the mobilisation?'

Tatischev, clenching his fists, could hear faintly but indistinctly the voice of the War Minister. For once in speaking to his Imperial master Sukhomlinov had lost his blandness. The Tsar listened carefully, but his face told his hearers nothing. Then he said, 'Very well, I shall replace the receiver, and very soon the Chief of Staff will get in touch with me. I shall wait here.'

He replaced the receiver and turned to Fredericks and Tatischev. 'The Minister says it is impossible to hold up the mobilisation. He says you cannot put the brakes on and off as in a motorcar. He is getting in touch with the Chief of Staff who will give me his opinion. He spoke very vehemently of the dreadful disorganisation if we try to hold up the mobilisation now.'

'Disorganisation more dreadful than war itself, sir?' asked Tatischev.

The Tsar gave him the nervous, meaningless smile Tatischev knew so well. But at least he was still holding his cousin's telegram firmly in his hand.

It was very quiet as they waited, quiet within the palace itself, quiet in the grounds too, for in July the giant fountains ceased playing at nine in the evening.

The telephone bell jangled. Janushkevitch, incredulous, appalled, still mentally reeling from the shock of Sukhomlinov babbling, 'Something frightful has happened! The Tsar himself has rung up—no general mobilisation.'

'That's technically impossible.'

'Good God, I know, but he insisted.'

'What in the hell's happened?'

'The Kaiser's put him on his honour.'

'What in God's name do we do?'

'*Nothing*. But it's up to you to convince him.'

Janushkevitch, still trying to gather his wits, was reduced to reading to his Sovereign excerpts from Dobrorolsky's memorandum on mobilisation. ' "The whole plan is worked out ahead to its end in all its details. When the moment is chosen one has only to press the button, and all begins to function automatically —precisely, like clockwork." But, sir, though it's easy to start, *once* we've started everything is settled, there's no going back.'

The Tsar, whose memory was excellent, repeated this to his companions. Tatischev said, 'It means that mobilisation determines mechanically the beginning of war.'

'That is what I, too, thought,' replied the Tsar, and resumed his conversation with Janushkevitch.

'The order for general mobilisation must be countermanded,' he said.

Fresh expostulation from the frantic Janushkevitch, the child facing the prospect of being denied the chance to put his clockwork toy into action. Would not His Majesty speak to the Minister of War again? He, Janushkevitch, would put the Minister through—

'At your feet, sir, I implore you!'—dramatically from Sukhomlinov. 'Your Majesty is making a terrible mistake! It's clear from the conduct of Germany and Austria that general war is inevitable. We can't trust the Kaiser—'

'I cannot accept that,' said the Tsar.

Even Sukhomlinov could see he had made a mistake. Verbally he grovelled. 'Sir, in my—my agitation I'm not choosing my words well. What I really mean is that we can't be sure that Austria will accept the mediation of the German Emperor. I am so upset, so confused—will not Your Imperial Majesty speak to the Chief of Staff again?'

Janushkevitch repeated his belief that, general war being inevitable, to suspend general mobilisation would only give the enemy a chance to mobilise more quickly than Russia.

The Tsar relayed this argument to his companions. 'It's our mobilisation that will make war inevitable, sir,' said Tatischev.

Old Count Fredericks did something quite extraordinary in

one so punctilious. Tatischev had heard the rumour that the old man called the Imperial couple '*mes enfants*' when he spoke with them alone; now the courtier said, very gravely to his Sovereign, '*Mon enfant*, the seconds are ticking away. There is no time left for argument. *Mon enfant, you are Tsar!*'

And the 'child' obediently said into the telephone receiver, 'It is my order that you countermand the order for general mobilisation immediately.'

Tatischev found himself furtively trying to rub his eyes. He caught the Tsar looking at him. 'Your pardon, sir, it's hot,' he stammered.

The Tsar shook his head. 'I've tears in my own eyes, Ilya Leonidovitch!' he said. He embraced both men, and made the sign of the Cross over them. Old Count Fredericks said solemnly, 'This is a great moment for our country and the world.'

'Go home and sleep in peace,' said the Tsar. 'We younger fellows still have work to do.' He turned to Tatischev. 'I must tell Her Majesty what's been decided—you can imagine how she's been feeling. Wait for me in my study, and then we'll send off a telegram to Berlin.'

Tatischev waited in the study with its tall windows overlooking the Gulf of Finland. The great gardens, the fountains, the distant river all seemed to sleep in a moonless pearly glimmer. 'It is—peaceful, isn't it?' asked the Tsar quietly, as he returned. He dismissed the servant who had brought two glasses of tea, a plate of the Osborne biscuits that the Empress, brought up by her grandmother Victoria, loved so much.

'Her Majesty is delighted, delighted!' he continued. 'She wants to see you before you go back tomorrow—but first let us send off the telegram telling the German Emperor I am sending you back to Berlin immediately.'

The telegram was sent out at 1.20 on the morning of July 30. It began: 'Thank you heartily for your quick answer. Am sending Tatischev this evening with instructions—'

'Come back at three this afternoon,' said the Tsar to Tatischev as the two men drank tea, after the telegram had been sent off. 'Get your things packed ready so that if need be you can set off straight from here. And now it's time you too went off to get some sleep. You have plenty of travelling before you.' And then, in a lower voice, 'What were you thinking as you stood by the window looking out?'

'Those lines of Shakespeare, sir:

> Upon the King! Let us our lives, our souls
> Our debts, our careful wives,
> Our children and our sins lay on the King!'

'Have you time to sit down for a few minutes more to listen to a story?' said the Tsar. 'It happened some time ago. General Orlov* went for some reason or other late one night into the room here where we receive petitions, and he heard this odd noise coming from the ante-room. He investigated and found a girl hiding there, crying. She knelt before him, saying her fiancé had been condemned to death, and was to be executed next morning. He was a student, who'd got mixed up with the revolutionaries, had tried to break away, but the other members of the gang wouldn't let him. "Already he has been sentenced to death by God," she told Orlov. "He has a disease of the lungs which will kill him soon enough." She had come to beg for a pardon, but her nerve had failed her.

'Orlov decided to take action, although it was so late. We were staying at the Alexandria Cottage; he got a troika and dashed over. I'd already gone to bed, but he insisted on seeing me. I granted the audience in pyjamas! I was glad he'd more or less burst in on me, and told him so. One must never hesitate to save the life of a man. I wrote a telegram to the Minister of Justice postponing the execution, and sent it off immediately, then told Orlov to go back to the girl and let her know what had happened. The poor thing fainted at the news. When she came round she said, "Whatever happens, we are ready to give our lives for the Emperor!" Orlov told me this in the morning. I said, "Well, you've made two people, the girl and myself, very

* Head of the Tsar's mobile secretariat.

happy." And if I felt so happy then at saving the life of one man, imagine how happy I feel now! This is one of the moments when one realises not only the dreadful responsibilities of power, but what happiness one can give.'

'Sir, on this occasion you have reprieved millions of innocent men,' said Tatischev.

'It is good not to have that on one's conscience. Be here at three o'clock then.'

As he drove back to his home in St Petersburg, Tatischev, in his moment of triumph, passed the General Staff building. Lights still burned there. In one of those brightly lit rooms sat Dobrorolsky, motionless. Tatischev's elation meant the other's utter dejection, tears of happiness at Peterhof, tears of vexation on the Neva Quay.

But others in the General Staff building and at the War Ministry were more resilient than Dobrorolsky. When Tatischev travelled out to Peterhof that afternoon, he did not travel alone.

His mood of elation remained with him when he arrived at the Baltic Station—rather, it was more keenly felt, being un-blunted now by physical tiredness. He had slept—long, dream-less sleep—booked his sleeping car—he had even had his luggage sent to the Warsaw Station *en route* for Wirballen and Berlin.

And then, at the Baltic Station, he met Sazonov, the Foreign Minister.

Tatischev thought, 'It is inescapable then.' That was what inevitability literally meant—something that could not be escaped.

'We are all, then, condemned still,' was his second thought, for Sazonov would be going out to Peterhof for one reason alone, to insist on general mobilisation. More, not being nor-mally due for an audience at this point, he must have specially requested the Tsar to receive him. And the Tsar, knowing the reason for the request, had, nevertheless, acquiesced.

A miracle had happened the previous night; the Tsar had asserted himself, and stood firm. But miracles rarely happened twice.

The two men scarcely spoke on the journey to Peterhof. It took just over fifty minutes, at first through meadows and forests, and then parallel to the coast-road, past the monastery of St Sergius with its miracle-working picture and so on to Peterhof itself, to drive past nurses with bright ribbon streamers, pushing perambulators, little boys cycling, old men sitting on benches dozing happily in the strong sunlight. And Tatischev sat in the motor in a cold sweat.

As they waited to be received by the Tsar, Fredericks came in. Sazonov was staring down at some notes he had taken from his portfolio, learning the lesson taught him by Janushkevitch and Sukhomlinov. Fredericks said to Tatischev in a low voice, 'It's bad. They've got at him. Telephone calls. Begging. Pleading. Russia's safety—honour. He didn't sleep much last night— too excited.'

'Her Majesty?'

'The boy's feverish again. *He'll* have to stick to his guns alone.'

Not a fortunate metaphor.

Tatischev, ushered with Sazonov into the Tsar's presence a few minutes later, was shocked by his appearance. The Emperor's face seemed covered with small wrinkles, wore an expression of helplessness.

The pleasant room with its tall windows overlooking the Gulf of Finland, the leather chairs, military pictures, tables covered with papers, became a room to be revisited in nightmare. Tatischev would always remember how the Tsar had carefully arranged the telegrams he had received from the Kaiser, and kept touching them, fingering them as a Catholic might finger his beads. A shaft of sunlight struck the desk. As it moved, so the Tsar inched the telegrams after it, so that always the light was on them.

But Sazonov, if reduced to the rôle of parrot trained by the

Staff, was a well-drilled parrot. For an hour he kept up the remorseless argument.

War with Germany was inevitable. If there were further delay, Russia would be in great danger, because the entire system would be completely dislocated by partial mobilisation.

What would France, Russia's ally, think of Russia's failure on this occasion? Would she not think it would be safer to stick to neutrality instead of relying on an ally who had shown herself unreliable? And would not the Germans, once assured of French neutrality, attack Russia?

The Tsar said in a stifled voice, clutching the telegrams, 'Are these the messages of someone bent on war?'

'Germany is only playing for time, Your Majesty. We must not give them that time. The order for general mobilisation must be given.'

'Think of the responsibility which you are asking me to take! Think of the thousands and thousands of men who will be sent to their death!'

'Neither Your Majesty's conscience nor mine will have anything to answer for if war breaks out. War has become inevitable. Diplomacy has done all that can be done. Your Majesty speaks of responsibility, but it is your supreme responsibility to think of the safety of the Empire—and this means meeting war fully armed and under the conditions most favourable to us. Your Majesty,' said Sazonov, a deeply religious, highly moral man, who, it was said, would have been an excellent candidate for the post of Procurator of the Holy Synod, 'it is better for us fearlessly to provoke a war by our preparations for it, rather than out of fear to be taken unawares.'

So it had gone on for an hour. It was four o'clock. From the sun-drenched parks of Peterhof the small boys would be cycling furiously home to tea, the nursemaids turning the perambulators round, the old men stirring on the benches. In the Tsar's study complete silence had fallen.

It was broken by Tatischev.

He did not mean to quarrel outright with Sazonov—that

would not help. He meant to begin by saying that there were strong arguments on both sides, and then to put the case for not ordering mobilisation.

But he got the phrasing wrong.

'Yes,' he began, 'it is hard to decide ...' In the instant he spoke he regretted the phrase, recalled what he had said days before, in this same study, of another Emperor; 'He's afraid of appearing weak—' was about to cry out, regardless of etiquette, 'For God's sake, forget what I've just said! I didn't mean it that way!'—only to find that the Tsar had already reacted as a man afraid of appearing weak might be expected to act.

'I will decide,' said the Tsar sharply.

And he spoke brusquely to Sazonov. 'Well, then, Sergei Dimitrivitch, telephone to the Chief of the General Staff that I give the order for general mobilisation.'

Sazonov rose, bowed, almost ran from the room.

The Tsar said, 'Leave me.' Tatischev did not look at his face. He did not think that the Tsar, either, was looking at him.

He went out into the corridor. From below he could hear the jubilant Sazonov speaking at the self-same instrument that sixteen hours before had been the instrument of peace. 'Now you can smash your telephone!' Sazonov, exultant, told Janushkevitch. 'Give your orders, General, and then—disappear for the rest of the day!'

Getting the three signatures this time was a much quicker business, but Dobrorolsky, who had not slept a wink that night, kept only a blurred impression of the interviews. His senses, however, quickened a little as he re-entered the Central Telegraph Office.

'Every operator,' he was to write, 'was sitting by his instrument waiting for the copy of the telegram in order to send to all the ends of the Russian Empire the momentous news of the calling up of the Russian people. A few minutes after six, while absolute stillness remained in the room, all the instruments began at once to click. That was the beginning moment of the great epoch.'

But it was not as it would have been on the previous evening. All his reactions seemed deadened, delayed, as if he were recovering from a bad illness. But did not Holy Writ say that hope deferred maketh the heart sick?

In the two and a half years that followed, colleagues and superiors noted that General Tatischev carried out the duties assigned to him competently enough, but without enthusiasm, almost automatically. The black mark against him was undue squeamishness over wounded; he would, for example, do anything he could to avoid being anywhere near a railway station if a hospital train were coming in. He had become taciturn; there were, in conversations with him, long silences and reticences, a feeling that his thoughts were withdrawn to a great distance. Possibly he showed less reserve in the company of his ninety-year-old invalid mother, to whom he was devoted.

He left his mother in the summer of 1917. Revolution had come six months earlier, and now the Provisional Government was moving the Imperial Family, for their own safety, to Siberia. The ex-Tsar was asked which people he would like to accompany him. The Tsar's first choice, Naryshkin, asked for twenty-four hours to think over the matter. On receiving this prevarication, the Tsar asked for Tatischev. Tatischev immediately packed his bag, and went to join the former Sovereign.

Had he known it, this was to earn him posthumous praise; he was one of the very few members of the entourage to show loyalty after the catastrophe. But he did not see his motive as loyalty; he acted as he did from a sense of expiation.

And so, with the Imperial Family, Tatischev learned what one of his fellow-captives called the psychology of the closed door and the fence. Only a prisoner could appreciate its significance. A door had once been something taken for granted, a useful object to ensure privacy, to exclude the unwelcome world, a protection. But now the closed door became a symbol of captivity.

The months passed, and more and more they lived under a prison régime, but that of a prison where there were many gaolers, each one of whom gave his own rendering of the rules set up by a drunken or sadistic commissar.

News came that Tatischev's mother had died.

In May 1918, the Imperial children, accompanied by Tatischev and other attendants, were taken from Tobolsk to join their parents at Ekaterinburg.

There is a last glimpse of Tatischev as he was taken to one of the prisons in Ekaterinburg. He said to the valet, Volkov, 'You see, Alexei Andreivitch, there's truth in the old saying, "Prison's like misery, you can't escape it".'

But perhaps, since that afternoon in late July 1914, he had not really tried to escape misery, misery was inevitable—like war.

The Bolsheviks shot Tatischev on May 25. He was told that he was being expelled from the Ural region and was taken out of the prison. A short time later the Cheka rang up the prison, demanding the money, some 5,000 roubles, that Tatischev had brought with him. The Prison Governor said he would give the money only to Tatischev, and was told Tatischev was already at the railway station, to which the Governor would not be admitted. Half an hour later the Governor received a formal order that Tatischev's money should be handed over to the Cheka agent who brought it.

At this moment Tatischev was facing the firing squad. The agent in charge of the shooting did not find it hard to decide to give the order to fire.

So Russia entered a war for which she was unprepared. In 1915, the Tsar took another disastrous decision; he himself assumed command of the army, leaving the real government of the country to his wife, 'guided' by Rasputin. At the end of 1916 some nobles murdered Rasputin, hoping to save the monarchy, but in a way they made matters worse. With Rasputin dead, all hatred was concentrated on the Tsarina, so detested and so much in people's thoughts that there was no need to mention her by name. She tried to rule Russia from her mauve boudoir in Tsarskoe Selo, outside St Petersburg, in an isolation broken only in such exceptional circumstances as when military cadets were summoned to provide a little companionship for the sickly heir to the throne, fretting against his confinement.

5
Incubation

Russia 1917-1920

He had, of course, taken the news home at the first opportunity.
His mother's reaction had been predictable. 'We shall be *made*!'
she cried, throwing her arms out in exultation.

'My dear,' said his father wryly, looking about their comfortable drawing-room, 'I don't think it can be said that we're—
as it were—unfinished!'

'You know what I mean!' she retorted, and, of course, they
all did, there was no real need for her to point out how, 'His
own cousins, the Grand Dukes' children, aren't invited to
Tsarskoe, so he must be desperately lonely and *wanting* friends.'

Then he was besieged by his sisters. 'Remember *everything*.
Not just what they say, what they wear too, and what they give
you to eat—'

'Of course,' he could hear his mother saying in an insuffici-
ently low voice to his father, 'if that vile creature had still been
alive—and possibly visiting Her—I shouldn't permit him to
go.' But then she was whisking about and calling to his sisters to
help with the great task of ensuring that his uniform was spick
and span as never before—'Yes, I know it's really Anna's job,
but she can't be in two places at once, and if we're to have sugar
and other things you know as well as I do she has to be queueing
for hours on end—unless one of you would like to take her
place!'

'Brrr! No, thank you, Mama!' they replied, laughing. Their
brother wondered for a fleeting moment how people managed
who didn't have a servant to queue for them. If it came to that,
if you were so poor you didn't have a servant, you probably had

to go out to work so had to decide whether you did your job or queued for bread, sugar, butter, meat, firewood. But if you *didn't* go to work, you had no money to queue with. 'How *do* people manage?' he wondered. Once he had voiced his wonder aloud, and his mother had replied indignantly, 'My dear boy, you sound as if you think we don't realise what a food shortage is, or how *terrific* prices are! Why, those last tins of biscuits from Elisiev's were absolutely exorbitant! I don't know how we'd manage without Papa's rations from the General Staff— and the poor dear suffers so much from the *indignity* of it all, having to walk across Palace Square returning salutes with his right hand and holding on to his little brown paper parcel in his left!'

Yes, he had seen his father besworded, gloved, immaculate, his face red with suppressed fury and humiliation. There was little expression on the faces of the thousands of badly clothed working women who stood huddled together for hours in the driving snow and sleet of the Russian winter, and often at the end went back home with nothing to feed their families, nothing to heat their houses—but were they not also capable of feeling anger, indignity?

He wished Rasputin, the 'vile creature', had not died a few weeks before, so that his mother would have refused to let him go. (But would she really have refused?) He felt quite sick with nerves at the prospect of the visit. One would, presumably, meet *Her*—everyone knew that even tough generals became so many bundles of nerves at the prospect of meeting the Tsarina.

The 'vile creature' might be dead, but they said She consulted His spirit at seances so His influence still dominated Tsarskoe—and He had been an agent of the Devil, some people said. A friend of his mother had written from Moscow that on the night He died it was said that priests in Moscow saying the Office seemed to go insane, yelling and blaspheming. In convents nuns had run along the corridors shrieking and howling like souls possessed.

No, he did not want to go to Tsarskoe.

When he got up on the morning he and the other two cadets were supposed to go he felt not only sick, he had a headache too, felt feverish. But he was told this was his imagination. He did not want to go, and so he felt ill.

In any case, even with the most splitting headache no cadet could disobey a command to appear at the Alexander Palace.

It took half an hour to make the fifteen-mile journey by rail from Petrograd to Tsarskoe Selo. They passed the Novo-Dyevitchi Convent on their right, and the aerodrome of the Aviation Battalion, then through fields and pastures to the heights of Tsarskoe. A car was awaiting them; they drove off, turned right, took the third street on the left, had a glimpse of the Catherine Cathedral with its five gilded domes, turned right again, and into the Palace Square, and there was the green and white of the great Imperial Palace, with, beside it, the smaller Alexander Palace, their destination.

The youngest of the cadets summoned to spend the afternoon with the Heir to the Throne felt more scared and sick than ever.

At least he could take some comfort from the fact that his older companions, for all their self-assured appearance, were almost as scared as he was. All three found the silence of the building unnerving. There seemed no bustle or movement. They knew there were servants and sentries everywhere, but no one seemed to come or go. Meanwhile they themselves stood in a white corridor in an upper storey of this silent palace; nervously, and in low voices, they ran over the careful instructions they had been given before leaving the Academy. Whatever the Heir suggested they might do, they must not play any kind of game that might develop into roughness. They were to address him as Alexei Nicholaevitch, his sisters as Olga Nicholaevna, Tatiana Nicholaevna, and so on. But above all, no roughness. They had not been told precisely why roughness could have such dreadful results, and this scared the youngest cadet more than ever. Everyone knew the Heir suffered from some mysterious disease that had nearly killed him more than once, but despite the wildest rumours, no one knew for certain what it was.

They only knew they must not be rough.

The white corridor in which they stood was divided into three sections by white enamelled wooden partitions. One section was full of toys, the second with dolls' furniture; this section had a notice: 'Admittance only with the permission of Olga and Tatiana.' In the central and largest section was a large table covered with French and English magazines; the eldest of the three cadets, trying to appear at ease, began to leaf through these. The second cadet, also trying to appear at ease, studied a neatly written timetable hanging on the wall. He whistled softly. 'They work them hard enough! Arithmetic, geography, history, Russian, French, English—'

The youngest cadet made no attempt at nonchalance. He stared miserably out of the window. Snow everywhere. Quite close a soldier in his long grey greatcoat pacing up and down. At some distance, a policeman in galoshes. Further away, beside the great iron railings, a flash of scarlet that was the uniform of a mounted Cossack.

He would have given anything to be able to press his hot forehead against the cool glass.

Beside him a voice said shyly, 'It is really nice of you to come.' And there stood the Heir, dressed very simply—a khaki uniform, long boots—but what struck the youngest cadet most forcibly—an impression so forcible that, unfortunately for himself, he was never able to forget it—was the expression of the grey-blue eyes looking up at him. It was only when he was older that he was able to find the proper adjective—appealing, no, more than appealing—beseeching. At the time he could only think of a wistful puppy trying to make friends.

All that he reported to his parents was that the Tsarevitch, although slightly built, looked much older than he actually was.

Alexei Nicholaevitch took the cadets to his own room. It was filled with mechanical toys of such complexity that even the two oldest cadets did not have to pretend interest. There was an entire railway system—level crossings, stations, signal boxes, trains carrying model passengers. There were armies of perfectly made model soldiers. There were towns, fortresses, factories with workers, mines with model miners descending and ascending, ships in a great tank.

'You just have to press a button,' said Alexei Nicholaevitch, doing so. The church bells rang, a few moments later the soldiers began to march, and then the ships began to move.

'Yes,' repeated the Heir, 'you simply have to press a button.' He gave a little shrug.

'May we, Alexei Nicholaevitch?' asked the oldest cadet.

'Of course; please do.' He turned to the youngest cadet. 'You don't seem so keen.'

The truth was that the youngest cadet felt so wretched that the thought of whirring machinery, the clanging of tinny church bells, the banging of miniature cannon was quite unbearable. But he could not say so. He could only smile and say—at a venture—that there had been some interesting-looking foreign magazines in the corridor.

The Heir's face lit up. 'Shall we go back there? I like cutting out pictures and painting them. You won't be bored? The magazines are very interesting, really'—and then, in a lower voice, and a slight jerk of his head towards the bell-ringing, train-whirring sound and spectacle—'much more interesting than *that* because you're doing something for yourself. That's fun the first few times, but then you get tired of everything happening just because you press a button. And you can read about what's going on in the rest of the world. Won't it be wonderful when the war's over and we can get out and travel? Papa says I'll have to travel a lot. Not that *I* mind. We went— oh, years ago—to England, a place called the Isle of Wight, and I went ashore and paddled and dug in the sand, and the girls went shopping—'

They left the two oldest cadets, fascinated by mechanical

marvels, and went back into the corridor. A sailor servant brought chairs for them. Alexei Nicholaevitch found water-colours and a pair of scissors in a drawer, they sat down, the youngest cadet in something of a blur of temperature and headache, and Alexei Nicholaevitch chattering.

'My sisters will be back soon—they go to the hospital every day, of course. They used to like it very much, but Olga gets upset now—no, not because of what they have to do, that I *do* know, but because of other things. I heard her saying once that the work's the same, it's the people who've changed—what do you think she meant? She gets depressed too when she goes into Petrograd for committee meetings, although she used to like those too. Still, it's enough to make anybody depressed, being a girl and not being able to get out much. At least, *I* can get out when I go to the Stavka* with Papa. I don't suppose I'll be able to go back this time—he's going back sooner than we thought he would, but he says it won't be for long, just a flying visit, and then when he *really* goes off again, I hope I can go with him.'

He talked on animatedly; the youngest cadet replied only in monosyllables, but Alexei did not seem to notice. His companion, for all his malaise, thought he knew the reason—Alexei desperately wanted someone to talk to. Confirmation came with the appearance of a silken-coated spaniel, whose long ears almost brushed the ground. 'This is Joy,' said Alexei. 'Have you a dog? They're useful when you need someone to talk to—but human beings are better, aren't they? Are you sure you're not being bored? There are plenty of other things we could do, although I'm not allowed to do anything like riding a bicycle or having a pony—'

No, said the youngest cadet with absolute truth, there was nothing else he wanted to do. Just to sit quietly cutting out pictures from the magazines.

Impressions became progessively more blurred. A man, a foreigner, Alexei Nicholaevitch's Swiss tutor, came and stood

* Russian Military Headquarters, at Mogilev.

beside them for a moment, explaining a difficult phrase or two
—'But I know the meaning of this one, *guerre à l'outrance*,' said
the Heir, 'it's war to the end, the bitter end, though I don't
know why the end's supposed to be bitter, it won't be bitter for
us, will it?' And there were the Grand Duchesses, the Heir's
sisters. A tall, slim girl—Tatiana Nicholaevna who stayed only
for a moment, saying, 'Mama will want me.' She was the only
one of the children the youngest cadet would have guessed was
the Tsar's daughter. The two youngest girls, Marie and Anastasia. Marie (Mashka, her brother called her) had immense
dark blue eyes, that was all the youngest cadet remembered of
her. All he remembered of Anastasia was her laugh—'She never
stops laughing,' said the Heir, laughing himself: 'She's an
awfully good mimic, too.' Marie and Anastasia went off to talk
to the two older cadets, and soon the boys could be heard
laughing too. 'She's very amusing,' said Alexei. 'You're sure
you'd not rather be there with them?'

No, he would prefer to be here, with Alexei and Joy, who
kept thrusting his cold wet nose against the visitor's hot hands.
'He likes you,' said the Heir. 'He'll know you next time he sees
you.' Then his face lit up. 'Here's my sister Olga,' he said.

Fair hair and wide-set blue eyes. A smile that changed to a
look of concern. 'Aren't you well? A headache?'

He stammered out, 'I'm—well, I was excited, I suppose. I—
I didn't sleep much last night.'

'You do mean *excited*, not scared, don't you?' asked the Heir.
'We're not *horrible*, you know. Whatever have you heard about
us?'

He laughed as he spoke, but his sister suddenly looked away.
Then she said with determined brightness, 'It'll soon be tea-
time; you'd better go and wash your hands, darling.'

While the two boys washed their hands the Heir apologised
in a low voice because it would probably be 'Only a very *plain*
tea. Mama said once she knew other people have more interesting teas, but it all goes back to Catherine the Great, you know,
we have to have the same kind of tea *she* always used to have—

hot bread and butter and saffron buns, although sometimes we have Osborne biscuits—do you know them, they're English, Mama loves them—and with any luck, since we've visitors, we'll get *biblichen*, little wafers covered with—what are they covered with, Olga?'

'Vanilla,' said Olga, who had just come back. 'Mama won't be having tea with us today, but she'd like to see your visitors before they go.'

'Papa?'

'It's a little too early for him—he says we must have it early, though, because he doesn't like to think of your visitors being kept here after dark, and it gets dark so early in February. But he'll look in.'

Tea was laid on small, white-draped tables. They drank tea from glasses with silver handles. There was the promised hot bread and butter, the saffron buns and the vanilla-covered wafers. The youngest cadet had never felt less like eating, but because of the Heir's delight at the sight of the *biblichen*, he tried to chew away. The Grand Duchess Tatiana was not with them, being still with her mother. Marie and Anastasia chatted and laughed with the oldest cadets, and had to be reminded by Olga that their mother expected them to get on with their sewing while they were having tea. A small puppy called Jimmy kept scrabbling on short legs to get up on to the lap of his mistress, Anastasia. Joy begged for titbits; 'You wouldn't do that if Mama were here,' said the Heir who was talking to the youngest cadet about his progress with the balalaika. Olga said little; she sat in the shadow; the youngest cadet could not see her face, but the droop of her head and shoulders showed weariness.

A slight, bearded man walked quietly into the room.

The oldest cadet, with a start, leaped to his feet, followed by his two comrades.

The Tsar of Russia, dressed as simply as his son, said in the very words his son had used—and, obviously, copied—'It is really nice of you to come.'

He could, he said, stay for only a few moments, but he talked a little to each of the visitors, asking their ages, saying smilingly, 'Well, I'm afraid you'll just miss seeing action, we're planning to finish the war this spring—you look disappointed, but it will be a good thing for Russia and the world.'

'*I've* been close to the front line,' said the Heir.

His father looked at him. 'But you didn't like all you saw, did you?'

His son flushed. 'No, I didn't, Papa.' He turned to the visitors and explained: 'We went to a front-line dressing-station in Galicia. They had only torches to give light. There were so many wounded there. And then, at a parade, Papa asked the men who'd been fighting since the beginning of the war to put up their hands. There were only a few of them—just a few to have lived through it.'

There was a moment's silence, and then Olga said from the shadows, 'Perhaps your visitors would like to see some of the photographs you've taken when you've been with Papa, Alexei.'

There was album after album, hundreds of photographs. The Heir brought out other albums, showing the Imperial Family relaxing on their yacht, playing tennis, romping with their pets, lying back soaking up the Crimean sun.

'Why don't they ever let people see *this* kind of photograph?' thought the youngest cadet. 'Then I shouldn't have been so scared of coming here, and I don't suppose I should have had this awful headache.'

Even She was smiling in the photograph of a picnic on the Finnish coast.

But She was not smiling when they were presented to Her twenty minutes later; even though the youngest cadet realised She was trying to, doing Her best to put them at their ease. She tried to smile, but the youngest cadet wished She had not; Her face was stiff (like cardboard, he thought) and it was almost possible to believe that the skin would crack with the effort of smiling. She spoke in short sentences, halting, toneless. She did not really seem to see them. Her eyes were tearless, not even red-rimmed, but the whole of the mauve room in which She received them, the mauve room so cluttered they were too scared to take a step for fear of knocking into something and sending it crashing down—this mauve room seemed to the youngest cadet to echo to the sound of weeping.

There was another lady with Her, Madame Vyroubova, pink-cheeked, round-faced. She talked to him too sweetly, too fussily. He didn't like her.

And then farewells were being said. 'If I don't go to the Stavka soon, you must come again!' said the Heir.

When they had arrived, the red afternoon's winter sun had burned in a steel-blue sky; now there was only a little pink sun-set left in the west, a transitory gleam on the lake they could see through the trees, a rosy background to the silhouetted rooftops of Tsarskoe before them. But it was the cold that came as a physical shock, after leaving the warmth of the great gallery, the scent of the hot-house flowers that were everywhere, the bright lights that had been brought into the gallery before they left. Now growing darkness and bitter cold, and an icy wind from the sea, bending the young pines and birches almost to the ground.

He felt quite dreadful, but at least he could report to his mother that the Heir had said, 'If I don't go to the Stavka soon, you must come again!'

He knew how she would respond. Once again she would cry, 'We shall be *made*!'

His mother died two years later in a hut in a Siberian village. She died of starvation. For some days before she died she had eaten grass, even handfuls of earth.

His father had been lynched by his own men.

He did not know what had become of his sisters. Sometimes he was glad of this.

He took part in the vain march by the White Armies to save the Supreme Ruler of Siberia, Admiral Kolchak.* One day of

* Handed over by the Czech Legion to the Bolsheviks, and shot by them at Irkutsk, in 1920.

119

that march he never forgot. It had begun for him an hour before dawn. Dawn with the hour preceding it is usually quiet enough anywhere; dawn with snow falling, either the big snow flakes of the west or the ceaseless, merciless downfall of tiny particles of the frozen snow of Siberia, makes for almost perfect silence—greater silence can be found only on the blue frozen lips of the dead.

The dawn of that day was unlike anything he had ever known. The sky, when it lightened, was the colour of sulphur, with great shreds and tatters of storm clouds, the kind of sky to herald the Day of Judgment. Had that dreadfully glaring sky opened to reveal God himself in fury walking on the wings of the wind down that lurid expanse, it would have surprised him for one reason only—because sometimes he did not think that God existed. Once they had retaken—for a short time—a town held and wrecked by the Reds. He had been billeted in the shell of a house whose unknown owner had possessed a substantial library. There had been a book lying open where it had been thrown down, trampled on; the muddied page had run, 'The old Sceptic Philosopher, Sextus Empiricus, said in his treatise *Arguments Against Belief in a God* that those who claimed that God existed, blasphemed. For if God is omnipotent, He is responsible for all the suffering in the world; if He is not responsible for everything, He is impotent.'

Then the noises had started. He thought that even if you doubted the powers of Heaven, you could not disbelieve that these were the shrieks of Hell itself, the sounds that could come only from winds roaring over vast distances, a thousand miles of steppe, ice, snow, shrieking of arid bleakness, cold, death.

As they moved off another sound was added to the pandemonium. As the sky screamed overhead, so the ground hissed beneath their feet, for any loose material—small stones, snow—those dry, frozen droplets of ice that march easily—was being moved off the ground by the violence of the wind.

And then the full impact of the wind reached them. It filled the air so full of frozen snow one could scarcely breathe, see—or hear. That was most amazing of all. They fought their way forward through a moving snow-drift so thick that it muffled even the sounds of Hell let loose overhead.

The storm had caught them on the flanks; if they had met it face to face they would have been finished. Even so, it seemed as if they would be swept off the face of the earth, but in the brief moments before the storm struck there had been frenzied commands to the few who rode to dismount and lead horses. Within minutes horses and men alike were hurled sideways, and the horses lay still, tethered by their heavy loads. The men clawed for what anchorage was within reach, and then had to fight another enemy, sheer primitive instinct to lie huddled on the ground until the storm passed—if it ever passed. But somehow, between gusts, they dragged themselves to their feet, tugged at rotten leather to loosen the horses' loads, and pulled them upright, then, but this time with two or three men on each side of each horse to hold him up when the next gust came, they plodded on again.

But at the end of the day, when they reached a village in friendly hands, there were dead and dying horses enough, dead or dying of exhaustion. Men in rags or stinking sheepskin stood at the heads of the shivering beasts who survived, de-icing the ponies' nostrils as they had to do every few hundred yards.

One of those who had been holding the village came up and said to the eighteen-year-old who had been the youngest cadet, 'It wasn't like this three years ago, was it? You're Grammotin, aren't you? I'm Argunov.'

Grammotin said, 'What happened to Krassin?' Nothing else seemed to matter but what had happened to the third member of the trio that had gone out to Tsarskoe that February day in 1917.

'Didn't you know? He was killed in the first days of the Revolution—he went to Church in his uniform, people told him not to, but he was proud of that uniform, and when he was going home some of the Red Guards got hold of him, ran him through with their bayonets and threw him into the Moika. His mother was with him.'

'He was fifteen and a half,' said Grammotin. 'A couple of months older than me.'

'You never heard of it?'

Grammotin looked about him. Brief day frowning into grey dusk with an immense sky the colour of iron, with a streak of blood in the west as there had been three years before, an immense snow-covered landscape, black lines of dead vegetation along high ice banks marking the frozen course of a river, black skeletons of trees, frozen sky, frozen ground, frozen blood on the dead, staring eyes and pale rigid faces. The broken howling of wolves had just begun and men were bringing out torches, bloody light again on the trampled snow, everywhere every day slow bloody dying on the trampled snow.

Yes, it was very different from the day when he had gone out to the warmth and stillness of Tsarskoe with Argunov and Krassin, Krassin who at fifteen and a few months had been run through with bayonets and tossed on to a frozen canal as casually as a farm labourer would fork dung on to the ground.

'You didn't know?' Argunov persisted.

'No,' said Grammotin, 'but then I didn't know much of anything that was going on. Do you remember that before we went out to Tsarskoe I said I felt ill and everyone thought I was putting it on? I wasn't, you know. Two days afterwards I went down with measles.'

Argunov gave a sudden exclamation.

'We were at different academies, weren't we?' said Grammotin. '*Ours* was moved to Ekaterinburg. I was one of the first to go into the Ipatiev House when the Reds had gone. I saw the bullet marks on the walls and the bayonet marks on the floor where they killed Anastasia. There was some blood left on the white wall. They were all murdered, weren't they, with their father and mother? The five children, I mean.'

'There were stories they'd got away, but those were put about by the Reds.'

'Yes, just some ashes in a mineshaft, that's all that was left of them,' said Grammotin, 'and I did my share in killing them. Because the five of them caught measles from me, didn't they, and so they couldn't be moved when the Revolution broke out?

'It's not everyone who just three days after his fifteenth birthday does for the Heir and four daughters of the Autocrat of All the Russias, is it?

'We looked after the dog, Joy; we found him there, waiting outside the door to their quarters. The others could never make out why I never talked to him.'

He turned away from Argunov, and led his pony away from the torchlight into the darkness.

6

A Time to be Born
and a Time to Die

I wish I had known Novgorod in the spring.

I went there in the autumn of 1916. It was a picturesque town of old wooden houses standing in gardens on the side of wooded cliffs, houses that were the homes of wealthy merchants who were lavishly hospitable. Their invitations meant pleasant evenings, for they and their families were well-educated, intelligent people.

What a pity, they all said, that I hadn't come earlier, in the spring, when the river was beautiful beyond description and, whenever you stopped when journeying along it, children offered you armfuls of lilies of the valley for practically nothing.

And in the bright moonlight, whispered the dark-eyed girls, nightingales sang.

And there were mushrooms everywhere, said their mothers more practically. Delicious ones.

They all said they hoped I should be in Novgorod in the following spring. Alas, I said, I shouldn't—I'd be taking part in the victorious spring offensive of 1917.

Then they hoped I'd come back when the war was over. It wouldn't be long now.

There was one family I remember particularly. A father, mother and two daughters, one twenty-six, the other eighteen, both married—and so, egoistic young brute that I was, I could relax in that household and not worry uneasily about saying or doing anything that might start ideas of matrimony.

To be quite accurate, however, although one need have no

worries in that particular respect in the company of the elder sister, Sonia, real relaxation still was difficult—Sonia being an extremely intense young woman. Fair hair, severely braided, a high forehead, wide, fervent grey eyes. She was the mother of two children for whom when there was company she would send in a challenging manner and clutch to her; knowing her to be a student of the classics, I used to wonder unworthily if she were inviting comparisons between herself and the mother of the Gracchi.

The appearance of Oleg and Kyril always imposed a feeling of constraint upon the company in general, since it was Sonia's frequently proclaimed intention to bring them up in the most enlightened fashion, which meant, among other things, that they were to see and hear nothing that was not beautiful and noble. 'No brutal words or ugly actions!' cried Sonia, which left visitors, before the children's round-eyed scrutiny, mouthing phrases of a strained niceness that the *Précieuses Ridicules* themselves might have found excessive.

The father of Oleg and Kyril I never met; he was a doctor, serving on the Galician front, a quiet fellow, by all accounts.

Nathalie, the younger daughter, was a little, laughing creature, her curling hair so fair it seemed almost silver. She was, said Sonia, soft-hearted to the point of idiocy (with the implication that Nathalie was soft-headed too). I remember a ludicrous incident on my first visit to their home. After a stormy night, it was one of those warm, drowsy days you sometimes get in October. Before lunch we sat in the garden on an elegant but extremely uncomfortable iron seat, and Nathalie, seeing a wasp expiring in a puddle on the path, tenderly fished it out, and put it on a rosebush to revive. It lay in the sun, the colour came back to its sodden body, it stirred, and then, presumably with the intention of showing it still had a shot in its locker, it briskly flew up and stung Sonia on the wrist.

Something of a scene ensued. It was not that Sonia was frightened by a wasp sting—any Roman mother could cope with *that*, while any good wife would enter fully into her husband's interests. She therefore dabbed away at the rapidly reddening swelling to the accompaniment of a clinical account of what was happening beneath the skin, but at the same time she was furious that this should have happened to her solely because of her sister's sloppy sentimentality. 'She couldn't say boo to a goose!' she kept exclaiming irritably, if not very relevantly.

Her anger was not assuaged by the sweetly maddening insistence with which Nathalie invited us to rejoice in the fact that the assault on her sister had been perpetrated by a wasp, not a bee—'So the poor thing won't die.'

Nathalie it was who, for all her devotion to fashion, bewailed the new styles with their slim, straight skirts, and no more puffed, beribboned sleeves. She adored the romantic English novels her sister denounced as trash; Sonia, of course, went in for sterner stuff. I remember that the moment before the wasp stung her she was earnestly telling me that she had just finished reading *Native Mysticism* by the Bishop of Tasmania.

Both girls spoke fluent English, having had an English nurse; the nurse being a native of Lambeth (having been born at no great distance from the home of the Archbishop of Canterbury, she had boasted to her charges) they also had unmistakeable Cockney accents.

I visited them for the last time in February 1917, four days before a telephone call from Petrograd gave news that meant the ending of the old world of Russia.

I went from the snowy street into the warm, lamplit room with the grand piano, the books, the embroidery, the velvet curtains, the thick rugs. Nathalie, in pale blue, had never been more vividly pretty; there had been a letter, her husband had managed to get leave, was coming next week—having heard her wonderful news. Her parents' mood was of mingled elation and the stupefaction they still felt that their little feather-pated Nathalie had married the son of a provincial Marshal of the Nobility. 'It makes Papa get all *dynastic*,' Nathalie murmured to me. 'He started to say this morning, "*What* a prospect for my grandson!" and Mamma shushed at him—he was being indelicate, she said. I don't think it indelicate, do you, Andrei Alexandrovitch? I think it's marvellous I'm going to have a baby!'

'To spoil, no doubt!' interrupted Sonia, overhearing her sister, and rather obviously torn between the desire to appear enlightened and her real feeling that this discussion of unborn progeny was indeed indelicate.

'I would love him as much as anyone could,' retorted Nathalie with sudden dignity, 'and do the best I could for him!'

But she ended the evening in fits of giggles, and I myself had difficulty in not joining her. The great question exercising her mind was what should she wear to meet her Igor at the station— would he prefer her in something new, or should it be something he had seen before, and liked. And, if new—

Sonia was contemptuous. *Clothes.* Here, as in other matters, she was progressive, to the extent of scorning corsets—as she had told me hardily. (This was not indelicacy on her part; it was a gesture against age-old tyranny.) If her sister would only read a decent book occasionally, she continued, instead of burying her head in fashion magazines and cheap, silly novels—

'Everyone can't be like you, reading Shakespeare all the time,' protested Nathalie. 'He's a genius, I know, but he's been dead three hundred years, and I like to keep *up* with things!'

Sonia picked up her copy of the Complete Works from a little inlaid side-table. Impressively she declared that although Shakespeare had indeed been dead for centuries—'You're unusually accurate, Nathalie; precisely three hundred years ago last April!'—what he had written applied as much to our day as to his. 'Frequently,' she concluded, 'if I have to take an important decision, I have consulted the plays and found guidance there.'

'What—like the *sortes Virgilianae?*' I asked.

'What do you mean?' demanded Nathalie, to exclaim after my explanation, 'What fun! Show us how it's done, Sonia!'

Sonia looked dubiously at her, but took the book, opened it

127

at random, dabbed her index finger on a line. Nathalie snatched the book from her, scrutinised the page, then gave a spurt of laughter. 'Oh, Sonia, Sonia, I *do* see what you mean!'

And, solemnly, in her high, sweet voice, with the Cockney vowels and lack of aspirates, she read: '*King Richard III*, Act Two, Scene Two.

'*Queen Elizabeth*. What stay had I but Edward? and he's gone.
Children. What stay had we but Clarence? and he's gone.
Duchess. What stays had I but they? and they are gone!'

Au revoir, Sonia, Nathalie, in that world where, if you were ill or hurt, you were cared for; if you were cold, there were warm clothes, heating; if you were hungry, you called for food—and it was there.

I met Sonia and Nathalie three years later after saying *au revoir* to them in Novgorod. I met them alongside what had once been called 'the route of civilisation'—the railway built across Siberia to the Pacific coast. I was retreating with the White Russian forces; taking part in the retreats of the old Imperial Armies in 1914 and 1915, I had thought that I should never know greater misery, but that had been only the first circle of hell, and I had been descending steadily ever since.

There were two highroads of hell, the iron road and the snow road, the railway and the *Trakt*, a track of trampled snow running alongside it. Those refugees who thought themselves the more fortunate had secured places on a train. But by the New Year of 1920, there was little or no fuel to be obtained. This meant that engines froze up, boilers burst, the train ceased to move. And if there were no fuel for the life-saving engine, assuredly there was none for heating the train. But those who had once fought and lied and cheated to get a place on that train now had a kind of superstitious terror of leaving it. Clawing themselves aboard, they had told themselves they had achieved salvation, and they dared not abandon the train.

So they stayed aboard, and mostly they died. Starvation, exposure, typhus—what did it matter? In the morning you would see the corpses brought out—if there remained anyone strong enough for this task. The bodies were stripped, even those infested with typhus-carrying lice, for any clothes were at a premium. They would stiffen quickly and remain so indefinitely in the icy air, so they were stacked in fairly orderly piles along the permanent way; having seen this often, even now I would not care to be near a timberyard in the evening half-light.

And there was the *Trakt*. Along the *Trakt*, even more so than on the railway, compassion was at a discount. The only feeling that seemed to survive in those still capable of mental or physical effort was the purely animal instinct of preying on the weaker animals. One rarely waited to plunder one's fellow creatures only after they were dead, although I can recall an elderly priest lying huddled in the snow and a peasant, judging him dead, beginning to strip off his clothes. The dying man stirred and groaned, 'My son, I am not yet dead!'

'Father, I will wait then,' said the peasant, respectfully rising to his feet and standing in attendance. But usually people did not wait. If you tried, by force or remonstrance, to prevent robbery of the dying, you received an astonished look. 'Why not? He (or she) is done for, anyway!'

Mostly, however, people simply did not notice what went on about them. Eyes fixed on the ground, this vast funeral procession of the old Russia dragged itself eastwards. It was no ordinary funeral procession, for those who moved in it knew themselves to be doomed, dying, carrying the seeds of death within themselves.

It was a silent procession. Each member of it had such an absorbing preoccupation with his own personal fate that there was no conversation between those plodding forward, no desire to communicate with those stumbling beside who had been friends, comrades, relatives, lovers.

As bodily strength weakened, brutishness increased. Bodies enough perished on that march; so, God have mercy on us, did souls. I have seen officers commandeer huts, barns, byres, for themselves, their horses, *their sledges*, while outside those sheltering walls men, women and children froze and stiffened in the darkness. On one occasion I saw strong men who had made a fire of fir-trunks, sitting down to brew coffee, roast horse-flesh—and then springing up to drive back with blows and curses a poor blind wretch who unwittingly strayed too close.

On my intervention a burly major, starting up to defend his sacred coffee-pot, upset it. 'Oh, my God! Oh, my God!' he shrieked in anguish, and burst into tears. I do not think any other spectacle had made him weep.

Against this background I met Sonia and Nathalie again. I had just clambered down from a truck in a stranded train. There had been a young woman dead in the corner, her head bent back, her eyes uplifted as if still imploring help not for herself, but for the baby one dead hand still clutched to her breast as a child might clasp a carved wooden doll. Her loosened black hair, moving in the gust of air when we had opened up the abandoned truck, was the only thing that stirred. The dead right hand was extended in entreaty. She had extended her right hand to me before, in a Petersburg ballroom in the winter of 1913–14. We had laughed because there were such mountains of food to be consumed, and after the second dance she had said, 'Let's sit the next one out—I must fan myself. This place is too hot, isn't it?'

I climbed down, and a voice spoke to me. I recognised her— just. Sonia. With one child.

'Oleg died of cholera when his father died. I wish Kyril had died then, too—cholera's quicker than starvation. Still, he's only a few days left—see, all the signs are here, the swollen stomach, the ulcer under the arm.'

The child stood like a docile, bewildered animal waiting for death. His face was like a wizened doll, his fingers literally no thicker than matchsticks. I was used to such spectacles now;

what horrified me was the fact that Sonia spoke in this way before a child old enough to understand what was said—the child who was to hear no brutal words, see no ugly actions.

'Where is Nathalie?'

'You want to see her? She went just a little way into the forest—not far, for she was weak.'

And ten minutes later she said, 'She had the baby in 1917. I wish I had her courage—she killed the little one because she didn't want him to suffer, and then she hanged herself.'

'*I would love him as much as anyone could, and do the best I could for him.*'

'*What a prospect for my grandson!*'

Lord, have mercy,

Christ, have mercy,

Lord, our God, have mercy on our Russia.

'To everything there is a season, and a time to every purpose under the heaven: a time to be born, and a time to die.'

Not in Russia.

No time to be born, only a time to die.

'And it is certain that the Old Gentleman had no conception of how terribly he had betrayed his trusteeship. He had only accepted Hitler on the condition that the Constitution should be respected and law and order maintained . . .'

Hindenburg, the Wooden Titan
Sir John Wheeler-Bennett

7

L'Après-midi d'un
Maréchal

(Germany, 1914–1933)

He took a little nap in the afternoon, because he must not be tired that evening.

'It won't be the same without you,' they had said. 'It won't be the same if you're not there.'

Not bad to hear that, when you were an old fellow who would have his eighty-sixth birthday in October. Eighty-six. The same as the old Austrian Emperor had been when he died. They'd called Franz Josef 'the Old Gentleman'. He'd heard they called *him* that now. 'The Old Gentleman.' 'We'll be all right with the Old Gentleman,' people said, and, 'As long as the Old Gentleman's there . . .' It was good to be trusted, to know that everyone realised it was his sense of duty that kept him going, had kept him going through three lives, if you looked at things in a certain way, three lives in one long life, one very long life, long enough for him to have chatted as a boy with an old gardener on his grandparents' estate at Neudeck—dear Neudeck—who had once worked for Frederick the Great. True, he'd only worked for the great king for two weeks, but even so!

'He gave us all this,' he'd told the gardener, meaning Frederick the Great, meaning Neudeck too, of course, Neudeck in the Neumark of Prussia, given to his family for services in the first of Frederick's wars, when he'd taken Silesia from Austria.

It was odd how these days it was easier to remember the face of the old gardener, the faded blue eyes, even a little triangular scar on the gnarled hand, than it was to remember who he'd been talking to only a couple of hours before.

When he'd had to give a reception to the newspaper men before he became President the first time at the age of seventy-seven, one of the reporters had asked him, 'What was the greatest day of your life, Field-Marshal?' and he'd replied, 'The first time when I was a cadet that I was allowed to eat as many cakes and as much whipped cream as I liked,' and after a moment's silence they'd all roared with laughter. Of course, they'd expected him to say, 'When I won Tannenberg.' Even in these days it really was hard sometimes to remember the details about Tannenberg—unless prompted—but easy enough to remember those cakes, the coffee icing on them, and the whirls of whipped cream. Yet today, oddly enough, it was different. Easy enough to remember quite a lot about Tannenberg. Was it because they'd kept saying, 'You must be there! It can't be done if you're not there!'?

And he kept seeing Ludendorff's face too. He hadn't been able to remember exactly what Ludendorff looked like for some months now. He supposed he hadn't wanted to; Ludendorff had been so appallingly rude at their last meetings. But now he kept seeing his face quite clearly. He wished he did not, because it wasn't the Ludendorff he'd first known, it was Ludendorff of 1918, Ludendorff of the sallow face, with the deep lines running from nose to the corners of his mouth, the corners of that small mouth pulled down (odd how he'd never realised before what a small mouth Ludendorff had). But above all, it was Ludendorff's hands he remembered. When Ludendorff was nervous, he'd sit absolutely silent at dinner, rolling bread-crumbs. If he rolled them slowly with one hand, he was just thinking. When he rolled them *quickly* but still with only one hand, he was worried, but, dear God, when he rolled them with both hands, his nerves were screaming inside him.

He hadn't noticed the signs for himself; at meal-times he concentrated on his food, not his dinner-companions' mannerisms.

135

It was Hoffmann who drew his attention to it. You never saw Hoffmann on edge. Rouse him a dozen times in the night with a crisis becoming worse, and he'd smile, tell his orderly to make him some Turkish coffee, pull out his silver flask in the meantime, take a sip of cognac, and then say, 'All right, give me the map . . .'

But of course Hoffmann hadn't been with them when Ludendorff was not only nervous but superstitious with it, and, which was even more trying for everyone if he'd known it, poor fellow, telling them all he *wasn't* superstitious. Those March days—in Avesnes, in 1918—Ludendorff was always looking into his little Moravian prayerbook with its texts for every day of the year. The day before the offensive he'd asked the man sitting next to him at lunch if he knew what the text was for the 21st? (That was a date one didn't forget, even in one's eighties.) ' "This is the day of the chosen people"—that's the text for tomorrow,' Ludendorff had said. 'We can't fail, then, to look forward to tomorrow with confidence!' Ludendorff was so excited when he spoke that he himself had heard it at the head of the table—couldn't make out why Ludendorff was so excited, and the fellow next to him with a peculiar look on his face didn't know whether Ludendorff was being serious or not. He'd had a word with him afterwards—von Tieschowitz, that was his name, his memory was improving every minute. He didn't want Ludendorff upset in any way. That's how he'd found out what Ludendorff had said.

After that it had got steadily worse. 'I am not superstitious,' Ludendorff would begin—to comparative strangers, sometimes. He'd had no confidence in July 15. Then he'd take out his little prayerbook and read out the texts for March 21, April 9, May 27, June 9—shaking his head all the time.

(There'd been that rumour that after the war he'd taken up astrology, dear God.)

Come, one's memory for dates was improving wonderfully, but must they be the dates that poor Ludendorff sat shaking his head over in those dreadful months in 1918? Make an effort, try to remember another date, when you first met Ludendorff, try, try hard, the day and the day preceding it—Saturday, August 22, 1914.

He had retired three years before. He'd been nearly sixty-five. His military career had carried him much further than he'd ever dared hope. There was no prospect of a war, and it was his duty to get out of the way to let the younger men have a chance. These were the honest facts; there'd been no truth in the mischievous rumour that his career had been affected by the unfortunate incident in 1908 when at the Magdeburg manoeuvres he'd let the corps commanded by the All-Highest lose the battle.

Retirement hadn't suited him. Retirement meant inaction, inaction of a particular kind. He hadn't sat down to be a vegetable; he'd travelled a bit, and hunted, and there was his picture collection, pictures of the Madonna and Child, he'd even enjoyed pottering in and out of the shops, and of course it was good to be free from responsibility, but—well, there was no getting away from the fact, retirement meant a part of one's life, the chief part of one's life, was over. His health began to crack; sometimes his dear wife would look at him, and he'd guess she was wondering whether he'd live to be seventy.

And then came August 1914. He only knew what he could gather from the newspapers. He'd sent a message to an old friend at General Headquarters, von Stein, 'Don't forget me if, as things develop, a commanding officer is needed anywhere,' never really expecting to hear anything as a result, but hoping and praying that they might find something for him to do, anything, and he meant it, for anything would be better than standing idle on the pavement, watching first the reservists walking through the streets to the barracks, wives, mothers, sweethearts surrounding them, thrusting parting gifts on them, a cake, home-made jam, sausages. And then the reservists would come away from the barracks *soldiers*, wearing field-grey, carrying packs, two blankets, a mess-tin, and rifles, and now the crowds pressed flowers on them, pinned them to their tunics, stuck them in their rifle-barrels, and everyone sang. It had been all singing and sun-shine and flowers at the end of July. He'd managed with an effort not to go to the station to see trains decked with flowers, filled with singing soldiers, pull out, east, west from Hanover, for the German forces were advancing on Paris and the Russians were advancing into East Prussia—as they had in the days of the great Frederick.

On Saturday, August 22, he had gone shopping in the morn-ing. Hardly any troops to be seen now; they'd gone to fight in the dust and heat, and he went shopping! The shopkeeper asked if his purchases should be delivered. 'No,' he'd replied, 'give them to me—I've nothing else to do. They don't want me now.' It was, he'd thought, the worst moment in his life. He'd almost envied the shopkeeper—he, at least, was doing *something*. What was there for *him* to do? Nothing but go back to the first-floor flat in the Holzgraben, and eat his lunch. He wanted to go out again—down to the railway station, or to buy another news-paper, but he knew that such obvious signs of aimless distress grieved his dear wife, so he'd tried to settle down with a book.

At three o'clock the telegram had come.

'What is it?' his wife asked, her hands, freckled with age, beginning to tremble.

'It's from Coblenz—General Headquarters. They want to know if I'm ready for immediate duty.'

'Where?'

'They don't say, but I'd better pack right away.'

He sent his reply, 'I am ready,' but packing had been a differ-ent matter. In the first place, he'd only had his blue peacetime uniform, and on Saturday afternoon there wasn't a tailor to be found from whom he might get one of the new grey uniforms for active service. And even his blue uniform—oh, the distress of his poor wife when, after they'd taken it out of the moth-balls and tissue paper in which she'd packed it away so carefully, he couldn't get into it! In a way it had been a good thing; what with letting out a seam here and there in tunic and breeches she hadn't any time for feeling nervous about the future, that very unknown future, for he had no idea where he was being sent. She was still letting out his tunic when the second telegram came, saying he was promoted to Colonel-General, that his Chief of Staff would be a Major-General Ludendorff, of whom he'd never heard, whom he would meet on a special train which would arrive at Hanover at four next morning—but of where the train would take him, not a word. It was only when he and his dear wife were agreeing in quiet despair that, do what they could, his tunic could no longer be hooked at the collar, that the third telegram had arrived. It told him that he was to command the Eighth Army in East Prussia.

He had told his wife, and she had become very silent. She realised how much depended on whether he succeeded or failed—that is, how much all Germany in general and dear Prussia in particular depended, for he must defend his home-land against the advancing Russians.

After a moment she said, 'I will come with you to the station. I am nervous, as you know, but I shall not cry.'

He had not been nervous at all, and he wanted to sing, to sing, 'Nun danket alle Gott'.

She had remained so nervous, he so excited, that they had gone to the station at three o'clock. He had tried to make her smile. 'See, the conquering hero—in uniform and boots not according to regulation, and my old *litewka* from the Third Guards!'

There were few people at the dimly lit station at this hour. Those who were looked covertly at this—well, survival, he sup-posed. He was eighty per cent embarrassed because he wore his old Prussian blue uniform, twenty per cent glad. Wearing Prussian blue he'd taken part in the triumphs of '66 and '70. Anyone born between the Russian and the French frontiers could wear this new field-grey. South Germans. Catholics. A sudden thought alarmed him—perhaps this unknown Luden-dorff wasn't a Prussian.

But within minutes *that* fear at least had been allayed. In came the train, in a shower of sparks—a toy train, engine, coal-tender, three coaches. Brakes shrieked, steam hissed, and a burly figure got down stiffly, his field-grey uniform seeming to mock the old *litewka*, and saluted—yes, that salute was reassuring, and so was the voice: 'Major-General Ludendorff, Your Excellency, by order of August 21 of the All-Highest's Military Cabinet, appointed Chief of Staff of the Eighth Army.'

The handshake was correct too.

And the face.

Yes, at that time he was convinced that Ludendorff had the face of a Prussian officer. He didn't think Ludendorff ever knew that once, when he was roused suddenly when the train stopped after a long journey they'd had to make to argue—at least, Ludendorff always did all the arguing, thank God!—about getting priority for their campaign in the East—well, he'd been roused suddenly, and couldn't think where he was, and there was Ludendorff, his face red with fury over some insult he'd been brooding over, and he'd had the most extraordinary moment of confusion when he'd thought Ludendorff was a pork-butcher in Hanover whose shop he'd passed daily in the three years before August 1914.

Once on the train, Ludendorff led the way to the third coach, the operations coach, and they had sat down before a swaying table to study the map. Ludendorff had done all the talking—after all, he was the man who'd received the briefing at General Headquarters. They'd sent for him to come to Coblenz from Liège. The All-Highest had been there, 'very calm,' said Ludendorff, but upset by the Russian invasion of East Prussia, and of course, the Chief of Imperial General Staff, von Moltke.

'How did *he* look?'

After a moment's pause, Ludendorff said, 'Tired,' then bent over the map.

That first conversation went on for only half an hour. Ludendorff had had a long day. At nine o'clock on the previous morning he had been notified he was to be Chief of Staff of the Eighth Army; Moltke had sent him a letter, 'You have before you a new and difficult task—I know no other man in whom

I have such absolute trust. You may yet be able to save the situation in the East—I know that you will not belie the trust reposed in you.'

Within fifteen minutes Ludendorff had packed, made his farewells, and was driving back to Coblenz in a staff car. He had reached Headquarters at six in the evening. At nine he had boarded the special train. With Moltke's consent he'd wired instructions direct to the corps commanders of the Eighth Army. The retreat to the west was to halt, and the First Corps was to move south by rail against the Russian Second Army.

Well!

It had not been difficult to put two and two together. He himself had received three telegrams, just sufficient information to start him on his way. No staff car had been sent to take *him* to Headquarters and anxious consultations for three hours. No letter telling *him*, 'I know no other man in whom I have such absolute trust.' Ludendorff had been issuing the essential orders while he'd still been trying to cram himself into his too-tight uniform. It was Ludendorff they'd looked to for snatching victory from defeat. He didn't mind that; he'd never pretended to be a genius, though he flattered himself he was shrewd enough. He was conscientious, dependable, and of enough seniority to carry sufficient weight to clear the way for Ludendorff's ideas.

How senior in years he was to Ludendorff had been made clear in an odd remark Ludendorff had made before their first conversation ended. *He*, feeling a bit of a fool because he knew so little about Ludendorff's exploit at Liège that had won him this great reputation, had asked a few questions about the Belgian campaign. Ludendorff had said abruptly, 'I shall never forget hearing the thud of bullets striking human bodies.' You remembered then something you'd forgotten—that this was Ludendorff's first taste of real warfare; *he* hadn't fought in '66 or '70. How many, indeed, had?

But after that moment of weakness, Ludendorff had shown only disgust and irritation when speaking of Belgium. Belgian civilians had broken the rules of war by firing on German troops. 'This kind of *franc-tireur* warfare is disgusting to every soldier. I found it profoundly disillusioning! The Belgian priests themselves were carrying stretchers, tending their wounded; some of our people shot them when they caught them doing it.'

His face had grown red with anger. 'The Belgian Government has a great deal to answer for! Innocent people have had to suffer, and they in Brussels are solely responsible! Do you know, Your Excellency, as I drove to Coblenz I passed through Wavre. Only the day before it was a peaceful town. Now it was in flames. Here, also, the civilian populace had fired on our troops! That was my last sight of Belgium.'

Even at that first meeting one had gained an inkling that perhaps what one was expected to contribute to the partnership was not only good sense, but good steady nerves.

So the train had thundered on eastwards, into dear East Prussia, its lakes and streams, its neat farmlands and small white villages won from forest and heath and scrub by Prussian toil and endurance. Time and time again they had passed crowded troop trains—all running west.

'We'll have to do the best we can until France is beaten,' he'd said to Ludendorff.

Ludendorff had said that should not take long. He described with animation how at Cologne he had seen the mobilisation plan in action; every ten minutes, regular as clockwork, a fully-loaded troop train had roared across the Hohenzollern Bridge. It had gone on like that for the first fourteen days of mobilisation.

At two o'clock in the afternoon they could see the red towers of Marienburg Castle. At Marienburg, filled with refugees fleeing before the Russians, the Eighth Army staff awaited them. And now one had cause to praise God for the superlative training of the German General Staff, for Ludendorff in Coblenz and Hoffmann, a Lieutenant-Colonel eight hundred kilometres away to the east in Neidenburg, faced with the same problem, had come up with substantially the same answer, and the orders given by Hoffmann had differed only in details from those issued by Ludendorff at Coblenz some time later.

As he himself had once said to Hoffmann some months later, with a General Staff that could keep those trains running at ten-minute intervals, not one a second late, and could train its officers so that two of them could hit upon almost precisely the same victory formula, any country was invincible. And Hoffmann, that odd fellow, had looked gravely at him, his blue eyes serious behind his pince-nez, and had said, 'It all helps to win battles, Your Excellency. It mightn't help to win a war.' But at the time he'd thought Hoffmann was joking. He was notorious for his sense of humour.

That was something else that he could remember with absolute exactitude, the circumstances in which he had first begun to think that Hoffmann, despite his first-class brains, might be not altogether reliable.

It had been in the December of 1914, after they'd established their headquarters at Posen, in the royal castle there. They'd got into the habit of sitting together after dinner at a round table, a great round polished table, on which stood a prized aspidistra, the gift of the Kaiserin, a true German woman, as Ludendorff frequently remarked. The Chancellor, Bethmann-Hollweg, had come on a visit. He was not an enlivening campanion; by all accounts he'd always been solemn-faced, but since the outbreak of war he'd gone around looking the picture of melancholy.

The snow had been deep outside; inside the castle the great wood fires blazed. The warmth and the brandy had made him sleepy; he'd listened drowsily to the discussion. They'd been talking of peace terms. 'If Germany makes peace without profit, Germany has lost the war!' snapped Ludendorff. Bethmann-Hollweg had turned his head to where Hoffmann sat sipping his cognac.

'And what is your opinion?'

And Hoffmann had replied, quite incredibly, 'In my opinion,

the first condition before peace can even be talked of is for Germany to declare publicly through *you*, sir, that it doesn't want to keep a single square of Belgian territory.'

There had been furious, inarticulate protest from Ludendorff. Hoffmann persisted, 'I say this because England will never tolerate a German Belgium, and will fight to the bitter end to prevent it. Besides, I do not think that an addition of Belgian subjects to the Empire is at all desirable for Germany.'

Yes, dear God, a German officer said this, sitting there in his field-grey with the little black and white ribbon of the Iron Cross (and he'd made a joke over receiving *that*; 'I never thought I'd get such a decoration through sitting at one end of a telephone-line.')

It was a relief to hear Bethmann-Hollweg saying, very slowly, 'You are the first soldier from whom I have heard this opinion. I quite agree with your point of view—but if I tried to express it in Berlin at the Reichstag, a storm of public protest would sweep me from my post.'

And quite right, too. War had been forced on Germany by a deliberate attack by Russia, supported by France and England. Was the Fatherland to seek peace from the warmongers, without ensuring protection against future attacks? Ludendorff and he had talked it over next morning, in perfect agreement. He'd felt it his duty then to have a word with Hoffmann. He'd said, gently enough, that he disliked seeing such mental short-sightedness in so clever an officer, repeated the arguments he and Ludendorff had gone over together. In return Hoffmann had talked confusingly of military expediency versus political advantage.

'Come!' he'd said, not quite understanding. 'You'd not dispute the views of General Ludendorff!'

Hoffmann had said, very quietly, 'A great soldier may not be equally great in diplomacy. He may be—well, let us say, too impulsive. A diplomat must know how to wait; a soldier wants something to happen immediately.'

Well, it was true that any kind of inaction had a bad effect on

Ludendorff. That winter and early spring, with a lull in the fighting, he'd enjoyed himself out in the open air, hunting, not with much success, alas, that being the worst of war, military operations cleared away so much of the game, but it was good to be out tramping through the forests, back to a good substantial meal in the evening, and then ten hours' sound, uninterrupted sleep. But Ludendorff, poor fellow, wouldn't stir from his office, was bored, restless, kept everyone on the run doing nothing. 'Work for work's sake makes it uncomfortable for everyone,' Hoffmann had remarked. Ludendorff grew sallower, and shorter in temper as the nights lengthened. His voice grew harsher, more rasping—unfortunate, that, because that tone of voice brought back recollection of an incident he didn't like remembering.

It had happened after Tannenberg, at the village of Osterode, where they'd set up temporary headquarters. (It had been gratifying to find himself quartered in the same old inn where he'd stayed as a subaltern during a staff ride in '81.) They'd captured a Russian general, Martos, commanding the Fifteenth Corps of the Second Army, a corps that had fought heroically before being shattered. Martos himself had been captured only after his horse was shot under him. He was no longer a young man, he had not slept for days, and had had nothing to eat or drink except for some wine and chocolate offered him by von François, a good Prussian general despite the name, who'd passed him in his car as he was being brought in to Osterode. He had lost his corps, seen his friends and comrades shot down all about him, knew already that his country had suffered the greatest defeat in its history.

Ludendorff and he had come to the inn together past thousands of Russians dressed in their green-brown uniforms, stumbling into captivity on bleeding feet. They were told of the captured general. For a few moments *he* had stood still, collecting his thoughts. What he was trying to do was to decide what to say to the poor fellow. One must not cause unnecessary distress to a brave fellow officer, who had suffered defeat. He must model his conduct on that of the good old Emperor, William I, towards the captured French Emperor after Sedan. What had the All-Highest done? He had done all he could to make the position easier for his defeated enemy, holding out his hand and saying, '*Sire, le sort des armes a decidé entre nous, mais il m'est bien pénible de recevoir Votre Majesté dans cette situation.*' (He, who knew no French, had nevertheless learned the words by heart.)

He had been so much engrossed in his thoughts that he had not noticed Ludendorff had left him. What roused him, in fact, was Ludendorff's voice, so harsh and rasping that it could be heard quite clearly, although he had closed the door behind him when he'd gone in to see Martos.

He was speaking in Russian, good Russian. His own Russian wasn't very good, but he could follow it.

'Tell me, what was the strategy of your famous General Samsonov when he invaded East Prussia?'

A tired, defeated voice answered, 'I was a corps commander. As such, I had only tactical tasks, knew nothing of strategy.'

'Yes, but now you are all defeated, and have laid down your arms. Now the Russian frontier is open to our invasion from Grodno to Warsaw.'

There was more spirit now in the answering voice. 'I was surrounded by superior forces, but before that, when my strength was equal to yours, I had considerable success against your troops. I had trophies—field-guns, machine-guns, prisoners —staff officers and many men.'

Ludendorff's voice became louder. 'Have you any money?'

'I have some Russian paper money.'

'That will be worth nothing now!'

He really could not let it go any further. He opened the door, and went in. There, in the dining-room of the inn, beside the empty white-tiled stove, this poor, beaten, exhausted, grey-bearded man in torn, stained uniform sat huddled on a plain wooden chair. There were two sentries with fixed bayonets inside the door—as if he were in any physical state to escape!

And, standing over him, hands on hips, Ludendorff. He'd never noticed before what short legs Ludendorff had in proportion to the rest of him.

He had crossed the room quickly. 'Hindenburg,' he said, and, as Martos straightened, then stood up, he put out his hand, and then—kind God, there were tears on the poor fellow's cheeks—put out the other hand too, took Martos' dirty shaking hand in both of his, and in halting Russian begged him, 'Don't worry, you must not worry.' Martos nodded. 'You will have your sword back as soon as possible.' Martos nodded again, kept his eyes fixed on him like a dumb animal desperately seeking the right reassurance. He kept on holding Martos' hand, praying—really praying—for inspiration, and, thank God, it came. 'You and your troops fought well,' he said. 'Bravely, and very well.'

Martos took a deep breath, tried to smile, said, 'I thank Your Excellency.'

Only then had he released the Russian's hand.

He had bowed formally then and, considering it best to leave the poor man alone, had made for the door. He had gestured to the two guards; 'Outside,' he said. 'No need to be in this room.' To Ludendorff he said nothing.

At the door he had turned and said quietly, 'I wish you happier days.'

He had never referred to the incident in any subsequent conversation with Ludendorff.

But, this apart, their partnership on the Eastern front held no unpleasant memories for him.

It had been different when he and Ludendorff had come to the Western front.

He had never been prepared for the first catastrophe. Defeat. In the spring of 1918 he'd been hopeful. He and Ludendorff had motored to the advanced headquarters at Avesnes—his first return to France for forty-seven years!—on March 18, three days before the beginning of the attack which would make the whole enemy line collapse. 'Closely connected partial blows,' said Ludendorff. The past few weeks had brought real spring weather—bright blue skies and fresh winds that dried the mud —but they'd arrived at Avesnes in the middle of a quite diabolical thunderstorm, and the next two days were days of heavy wind and lashing rain. On the 21st it was foggy; the sound of the massed guns firing from four in the morning along seventy kilometres of front was only a distant rumble, but he and Ludendorff had put on their helmets, and taken their ceremonial swords to pose before headquarters for the photographers. And at first the news had been good, very good. *He* had gone on being hopeful through the summer. But then had come the dreadful afternoon in September when they had come to tell him that Ludendorff in his room one floor above, on receiving news of fresh successful enemy counter-attacks, had got unsteadily to his feet like a drunken man, and had shouted curses against the Reichstag, the civilians in the rear, the Navy—*the All-Highest*. 'He is in a frenzy,' they said. He could only say, 'Get his doctor, and then tell the doctor to come to me.'

What had the doctor said? 'His work has been his life. He has had neither eyes nor ears for anything else. He has never seen a flower bloom, never heard a bird sing, never watched the sun set. He needs treatment *for his soul*.'

And at six o'clock that evening there had been slow footsteps coming down the stairs, and then, after a pause, a knock on his door; Ludendorff with a sick white face, his whole body shaking. For a long time they'd looked at each other without speaking, and then, slowly, haltingly, as if he were speaking a foreign language he had only just commenced to learn, Ludendorff said, 'We shall have to ask for an immediate armistice. We have no reserves.'

He had stood up then, and taken Ludendorff's right hand in both his own, and suddenly he had remembered Martos' despair in that inn at Osterode, and Ludendorff standing over him.

Was that September afternoon the worst in his life, or had those November events that left the Empire without a Kaiser, the Army without a War Lord, been even more terrible? The All-Highest must abdicate, must get across the border into

Holland if he were to escape the fate of his Russian cousin, but he could not tell him so. Because inevitably the All-Highest would reply, 'There's trouble in Berlin, but the Army can deal with *that*,' and he, a Prussian officer, could not tell him that the Army itself had turned against its War Lord.

That day, too, had been foggy.

He had told Gröner he would have to do it. Gröner, who had taken Ludendorff's place, came from Würtemburg; the military tradition was different there; he might say what a Prussian officer would find unsayable.

They had spoken to the All-Highest in a room overlooking the garden. It was inadequately heated by a wood fire. The All-Highest leaned against the mantelpiece, shivering.

He could not remember all that had passed. Gröner had given facts, and summed up—there was no reliance on the Army, it would not go on fighting.

One courtier had said something about subduing mutiny by smoke-bombs, gas and flame-throwers.

The All-Highest still did not understand. He had said he would stay quietly here until an armistice had been signed, and then go home at the head of his Army.

Gröner said quietly, 'Sire, you no longer have an army. The Army will march home in peace and order under its leaders, but not under the command of Your Majesty—'

'Have they not taken the military oath to me?' cried the All-Highest, and Gröner had replied slowly, and sadly, 'Sire, in such a situation the oath of loyalty is now only a fiction.'

He could remember nothing more that had been said. They had gone out in wretched little groups through the french windows to walk in the fog among the beds of withered flowers. Thank God he'd been able to go back to his quarters then, instead of going into the bright white room with the others where luncheon was laid on flower-decorated tables. He didn't know whether they'd managed to swallow anything.

Odd that he and Gröner had after all that wretchedness eventually become officers of the Republic, he as President, Gröner as War Minister: Paul von Hindenburg at seventy-eight becoming President of a Republic! But he had only consented to the idea because people had convinced him it was his duty. Once again Germans were looking to him to emerge from retirement to save them. If the Fatherland were in such danger, and only he could save it, he had no right to refuse. So he had agreed, making one stipulation. He had been horrified to find in the newspapers supporting the rival candidate quite appalling personal attacks on himself. He had said to his supporters that there were to be no reciprocal slanderous campaigns against his opponent. 'I will not allow such things to be said on my behalf. I insist upon my political opponents receiving fair play from my supporters.' A great pity that somehow there was a fault in the lines of communication and the mud-slinging had continued.

Well, he had been elected, and the bewildering years had followed. Chancellors came and went; he could never really understand why they so frequently had to resign. 'Why did he go?' he asked once. 'He was quite a nice man.' 'Yes, Your Excellency, but he couldn't find a majority.' 'Oh, well, he suited me very well, but if they want a new one I don't mind.' And then, after a moment, he thought it better to explain, not for the first time, 'You see, no one could be less of a politician than I am.' 'Yes, Your Excellency.' 'All that I wish to do is serve the Fatherland—is that understood?' 'Yes, Your Excellency. Everyone understands that.' He hoped they did.

They must have, because they elected him a second time—at eighty-four. How his countrymen had trusted him, and how he had striven to justify their trust—but a man of eighty-four could not help wishing that people would sometimes remember his age and not pester him quite so much.

He had said to Gröner one day, 'How old are you, Gröner?'

Gröner had said he had been born in 1867. 'Quite. Twenty years younger than me. Born the year after I rode behind the

Emperor William I—King of Prussia in those days—through the Brandenburger Tor after the war against Austria.'

He began to think happily of that war. His baptism of fire at Soor, and then the capture of the battery of guns at Königgrätz that had won him the Order of the Red Eagle.

'It must be suppressed. An absolute private army,' Gröner was saying, as he said so often these days, which was why one didn't have to concentrate to follow what he was saying. 'A danger to the State—'

He said sleepily, 'Not so great a danger as Communism, Gröner.'

'More of a danger, Your Excellency. Because the Army will always defend the Fatherland against Communism. I am not so sure of the attitude of younger officers to *this* movement. Its newspapers are openly inviting the Army to repudiate its oath to the Republic—the military oath has been broken before.'

Gröner was looking miserable again. He said briskly, '*That* fellow a threat, Gröner? You know, the first time he got himself talked about, that Munich buffoonery, Admiral von Hintze was there. You know Hintze—'

'Yes, Your Excellency. Foreign Minister in 1918.'

'Quite. Well, *he* was there in that Munich beer-hall when the fellow jumped on the table, started shouting and waving his arms about in his shockingly fitting morning suit, and all that Hintze could think, so he told me, was, "The poor little waiter!" Now, Gröner, we know, strictly between ourselves, that one of the reasons people told me I ought to stand for re-election was that it was quite impossible that I, a Field-Marshal, should make room for this Bohemian corporal—'

'Austrian, Excellency.'

'Well, not even German-born. He had to get citizenship somehow or other before he could stand for the election. I've met him, you know, didn't care for him at all. A few young fools among the junior officers may be impressed, but not the rest, and if he tries to make trouble, the Army'll take care of him. Good God, the Army's taken care of bigger men than him in the past!'

He had regretted that Gröner, after his resignation, hadn't been able to see the interview he'd given the Bohemian corporal and one of his cronies last August. He had not offered them chairs, made clear his contempt in a dressing-down in a good carrying parade-ground voice for fifteen minutes, and then got rid of the precious pair with a recommendation to use a little chivalry in future campaigns. 'That man for a Chancellor!' he'd said in a ringing voice after the door had closed behind his visitors. 'I'll make him a postmaster, and he can lick the stamps with my head on them!'

Someone coming in to disturb his thoughts, give him details of the procession tonight. The Stahlhelm, the ex-servicemen's organisation would be marching—good, they still marched well, with the old snap and swing, wonderful what putting on the field-grey again could do for a man. Before them the Brown-shirts. Had he said something then, or simply looked up in a certain way, so that people gathered round him, saying quickly, 'Yes, by doing *that* you've saved Germany again!'

He had been very tired for a long time. Any other man was allowed to give up when he became old, but not Paul von Hindenburg. But even Paul von Hindenburg could not go on for ever. He had instructed his doctor to be perfectly frank with him when the time came, when death was close at hand, not quite in the room, but approaching the house. 'I want to know, Sauerbruch, so that I'll have time to confer with the Lord a little. Then you may tell Friend Death he can come in.'

Yes, he was very tired, and the responsibilities were very great. That was why he had been glad when they had talked to him about the Enabling Bill, which would relieve him of so many burdens. 'Let the Chancellor shoulder the load for you. He will do all that you have always wanted to do!' Voices had talked of wiping out the old stain of November 1918; defeated, shamed Germany would grow strong, proud again. He had said—he could not control his tongue now as he had once been able—something confused about the other stain of November 1918, not only defeat, but the breaking of the oath to the War Lord, the King of Prussia. 'Yes, with a strong Chancellor, restoration of the monarchy, your old secret dream, will be possible too.' Or had they said this before he had appointed that Bohemian corporal as the new Chancellor? He could not remember. And he could not remember, because he tried not to remember, when exactly they had told him that only a government headed by this new man was prepared to suppress an investigation—kind God, it hurt to remember it—into the corrupt use of public money by certain landowners in East Prussia.

He had written to his wife in July 1918 that if the war was not won, it would not be his fault, but because of Germany's lack of spiritual strength. There had been no spiritual strength in Germany for years now. He'd noticed the changed expressions on people's faces. A sharpened look. Suspicious. Sometimes jeering. If this new man could indeed bring the old Germany back, where oaths had not been mere words, his appointment would indeed be the last great service to the Fatherland.

They had roused him, and washed his face, brushed his hair, spruced him up generally. They said again to him, 'You are saving the Fatherland in peace as you saved it in war.' These days he could really remember only the last thing people said to him. He stood before a window, closed, because the damp January night air must not hurt him. There was a great torchlight procession below, rank after rank of men in grey, marching with military precision, and, before them, men in brown moving with no precision at all. He had been very happy, standing there, beating time with his crooked old walking stick to the music of the military bands, but now he was indignant. Good God, what were they thinking of, letting this lubberly crew shamble along the Wilhelmstrasse? He tried to say something, and immediately the voices said, 'You have saved the Fatherland, Field-Marshal,' and suddenly he understood. That day when he'd talked to Martos—brown-clad men plodding unsteadily into captivity on bleeding feet. He called out exultantly to the partner in his triumph, who must assuredly be standing behind him, and not looking puzzled, uncertain, as he had in those later, dreadful days, 'Ludendorff, how well our men are marching! And what a lot of Russian prisoners they've taken!'